A.D. BRAZEAU

Evernight Teen ®

www.evernightteen.com

THE ENCHANTING RISE OF MIRANDA STONE

Copyright© 2023

A.D. Brazeau

ISBN: 978-0-3695-0903-1

Cover Artist: Jay Aheer

Editor: Melissa Hosack

A.D. BRAZEAU

DEDICATION

For all the women fighting for what's right—we are stronger together.

A.D. BRAZEAU

THE ENCHANTING RISE OF MIRANDA STONE

The Emergence Duology, 2

A.D. Brazeau

Copyright © 2023

Chapter One

The Taos sun was hot. The heat here was dry, so I could warm myself in it without turning into a puddle.

I leaned back in the cracked, plastic lawn chair, sure to fall on my ass any second and not really caring. Even after sleeping a full ten hours, passed out like the dead, I was still tired, dread rolling through me at the thought of another long day stuck in the car.

We'd driven straight through to New Mexico the previous day, finally stopping for some rest at midnight. Without speaking, the three of us—me, Billie, and Neeta—had rented the filthy, street-side room with cash from our stash, taken turns in the shower, grout grungy and peeling, then closed our eyes against the fear, the panic, and the pain of leaving loved ones behind.

There was no time to think of what we'd left, of whom. There was no time and no room in our shattered brains and hearts. There was only survival.

I was the first one up, the first one to grab a bag of chips from the pathetically stocked vending machine. It was a cheap breakfast that wouldn't break the bank. I was then the first one to repack my suitcase, given to me by Ruby before we left, ready to get on with what was sure to be a long day.

I looked over the note I'd written Ash the night before on the motel's cheap, yellowing pad of paper. One of the things that had struck me about her in the first days—aside from the fact that she was hot as fire—were the little notes she wrote to me. I thought returning the favor while on the road might give me something other than dread to focus on.

Ash, I'm not good at this writing thing, expressing myself through my own words. Ask me to serenade you with a song written by someone else or ask me to put together a killer playlist, and I'll sweep you off your feet. I don't even know if you'll ever read this, but I'm sorry and I love you.

The note wasn't much, but it was all I had to give at that moment.

The parking lot was half full, and as I munched on the bag of broken, stale chips, I scanned the area, always on alert for anyone who may wish us harm.

One couple was packing up their car, looking as weary as I felt. I watched them for a moment, then turned my attention to a man who'd just come out of a room directly across from ours. He closed the door behind him, then leaned against it, pulling a pack of cigarettes from the breast pocket of his shirt. He popped a cigarette in between his lips, then tugged out a lighter that had been stuffed inside the crumpled box alongside the smokes.

He cupped his hand around the flame. As he inhaled, he glanced up and over at me. His gaze lingered on mine a beat too long, causing a twinge to dance in my belly. I tried to take him in while appearing to gaze off to the side. I kept him in my peripheral, careful to take in as many details as possible.

I didn't like the look of him. There was something haunted in his eyes that was plain to me even across the parking lot. The flesh around his eyes was dark, bags the size of New Jersey underneath, and saggy like a bloodhound. He reminded me of an actor playing the part of a private detective, someone grizzled and tired, always on the hunt for one person or another. His clothes had the rumpled look of being slept in.

I wasn't one to judge, I was sure I looked just as bad, my hair washed but pulled starkly back, my face free of makeup, my jeans and tank top as nondescript as possible. Still, I righted my chair, my gaze now locking with the man.

Breath caught in my throat. It was the way he didn't look away that alarmed me the most, made me feel as if he were trying to figure something out, maybe trying to calculate his odds.

The door to our motel room opened, causing me to almost flinch in surprise. The chair shifted in the dirt with a crunch.

Out stepped Neeta, her backpack in hand. "Let's get the hell out of this place," she said, breezing by me to walk the ten steps to the car her mom had given us. Crystal, Neeta's mom, had insisted we take her gray SUV as the three of us made our escape out of New Orleans toward a future none of us were certain of.

Neeta wore a backward baseball cap over her braids, a hoodie on over shorts, even though the temperature must have been somewhere near one hundred degrees.

My attention snapped back to the man across the way, but he was nowhere to be seen. Cold fear washed over me. I cursed myself for not paying closer attention. The guy could be anywhere, back in his room, in his car waiting to follow us, making a phone call to the police. I looked every which way, squinting into shadows.

The chair I'd been sitting in toppled as I scrambled to my feet.

Billie came rushing out the door next, her pink duffle and my suitcase in her hands. "I'm with Neeta. This place is giving me the creeps. It's so dusty and quiet, even though it's right off the road. I mean, how weird is that?" Billie didn't speak to anyone in particular as she threw the bags in the open back of the SUV.

"Traffic is light everywhere, which is very weird, yes." Neeta adjusted her cap.

Still standing with my half-eaten bag of chips in my hand, I re-scanned the lot. Smoking guy was nowhere to be seen.

"What's going on?" Billie slammed the back of the SUV closed, her short blonde hair smashed against one side of her face. The jeans and cropped t-shirt she wore were wrinkled from being stuffed in her duffle. "Miranda."

I edged toward the driver's side, still looking around. It was my turn to drive. "I don't know. Maybe nothing, probably nothing."

Billie jumped into the backseat without saying a word, Neeta standing on the opposite side of the car, the passenger door held open as she, too, glanced around us. "Just get in, Miranda. Billie's right, this place is weird. This motel makes the Fleur de Lis look like a damn palace."

Every place was weird anymore. There was no escaping it. We were two young women and one teenager, on the run from a threat we couldn't even name. I was pretty sure nothing would ever feel normal again.

I slid into the driver's seat, ready to leave the heat of the southwest behind, ready to leave behind most everything, everything except the people we'd left in New Orleans—the friends, the family, the lovers, people who I wasn't sure we'd ever see again.

What awaited us in Colorado was as mysterious to me as the arrival of my powers had been. There were moments when I wondered what would happen if the three of us just found some shack out in the middle of nowhere, some hole we could hide in until the day when, maybe, this would all blow over. But thinking that way felt a lot like giving up, like pedaling backward. There was only one way in all this, and it was forward. Forward, for some inexplicable reason, was toward the mountain town of Estes Park. In that haven, we would find either solace or, if something had happened to my aunt, another nightmare, and there was only one way to find out. We had to keep driving.

Chapter Two

Driving through Walsenburg, Colorado, my stomach began aching. The terrain was flat and uninspiring, the town old, as quiet as the roads thus far had been.

An hour and a half until Colorado Springs.

I swallowed bile, my stomach, long empty of the chips I had for breakfast, seemingly twisting in on itself.

"What's wrong?" Neeta asked, perking up from her half-reclined position to look over her shoulder, out the back window of the now dusty SUV.

Billie was sprawled over the length of the backseat, a magazine she'd stolen from the motel, and wasn't reading, open in her lap.

"No one's behind us," I said, rolling my neck in a circle as I drove. I didn't know it was possible to feel so stiff at sixteen. "I'm hungry, and I'm scared about driving through the Springs. What if someone I know sees me?"

"Probably not likely," Billie said as she flipped the pages of her magazine without looking at them. "Isn't Colorado Springs a pretty big place? But we should take every precaution. Why don't we pull over, grab some food, and I'll drive the rest of the way? It's my turn, anyway, and I'm bored. Driving will give me something to do." She tossed the magazine onto the floorboard. It was littered with what I knew to be half eaten bags of chips, candy, and beef jerky.

I didn't need to be told twice, taking the first exit I saw. All the driving was exhausting. I'd rather stare out the window or try to close my eyes for a little nap. A fast-food place promising southern Colorado's best green chili burger sat on the corner. I parked and we went inside as one unit.

We'd been nothing but a single unit since leaving New Orleans. When we stopped for gas, we all got out of the car, standing near each other, each one guarding the other. When we went in to pee, we went together, all three of us hitting the restroom at the same time, even if there was only one stall. These things happened without a word; they were agreed upon on a subconscious level. Not one of us would be alone, not until this was over.

Inside the restaurant, the smell of grease from the fryers hit me hard. I wasn't sure if I was still hungry or if I was about to now be sick.

We ordered, hit the restrooms, then grabbed our bag of oily food. There was no luxury of time, and there wouldn't be until we made it to Estes Park. The longer we were stopped at any one location the more likely we were to be picked up. If we were wanted, which I was pretty sure we were. After the events at the Fleur de Lis, how could we not be? I still didn't know what happened to Henry. He could be dead for all I knew.

Can't think about that right now.

I took up the back seat, so I could hit the deck once we made it to the Springs. It would take twenty minutes or so to clear my hometown, and I would feel more comfortable out of sight.

Yesterday, the long drive from New Orleans to Taos had been one of relative calm. After what we'd been through with Henry, and after the emotional goodbye we'd been forced to say to our loved ones, all three of us had been quiet, numb almost, as if every last drop of feeling had been wrung from us, left behind. This was a good thing as far as our powers were concerned. In that numb state, the powers would lay dormant, locked away out of sight. Although we had improved control over the magic, we were still figuring everything out, still aware that we knew very little.

Now, I could hardly sit still. Colorado Springs was an hour and a half away. Bouncing in my seat as I ate, fries crunching in my half-open mouth, I tried thinking of anything other than what it would feel like to drive through the city where I'd spent my life, the city I'd run from, the family I'd run from. This kind of nervous energy was dangerous. This kind of feeling could bring the powers out. The last thing any of us needed was to bring attention to ourselves before we made it all the way north. Worse than that, we could do real damage to ourselves were the energy ignited while we were driving.

I took a ragged breath, then another, as I tried to calm my mind.

Naturally, my thoughts moved to Ash. In my mind, Ash's beautiful face lit up with her bright smile. Her soft lips grazed my shoulder, her laugh, infectious, which made me think of angels sitting on clouds. A pang in my gut nearly brought up the fries. I swallowed, gazing out the window at the barren fields flying by.

More than once since we'd escaped I had wondered if I'd made the right decision by leaving her behind. As she was, Ash was safer at home, safer with her mother and everything that was familiar to her. But what if she started developing powers of her own? If she did, and something terrible happened, I would never forgive myself.

I squeezed my eyes shut.

Less than five hours to go. Keep it together.

Opening my eyes, I focused on the back of Neeta's headrest as she shoved fry after fry into her mouth. Hunger was another problem that brought our powers to the fore. Even though we'd done a pretty good job of learning how to control the energy, there was still the possibility of hell breaking loose. It wouldn't have been the first time. We could all attest to that.

Neeta reached out a hand to play with the radio.

Billie took one hand off the wheel to swat her away. "We said no radio, not until we get there."

Billie was right. We'd agreed to cut ourselves off from any news that might disturb, any news that might upset.

"I just want to listen to some music. The silence is killing me. I'll find a good station, don't worry. It's not like some local pop station is going to have serious news reports." Neeta continued pressing the screen of the control center until she found a station we could live with. There weren't many options.

The country station was far from ideal, but at least, to Neeta's point, the twangy inflections would be better than listening to my thoughts.

As the female singer ended her song about her cheating husband, the DJ came on to announce a contest for concert tickets.

I was anticipating another song or maybe an advertisement, when the DJ said this, "Twelve more Colorado women have been detained following a worldwide surge in what some are calling witchcraft. While we at KROW are withholding judgment at this time, it is prudent to take precautions. Whether these women mean to do harm has yet to be determined. So, fellow Coloradans, proceed with caution. I've no doubt our local and national authorities will get a handle on the situation, and all will be resolved. No need for panic or alarm."

With a flick of her finger, Billie turned off the system.

We continued on in silence for several miles, food forgotten.

Finally, Billie said, "No need for panic, my ass. Easy for him to say. A male DJ who has nothing to fear.

We're the ones who…" Billie's voice died in her throat.

"We're the ones who are in fear for our lives," Neeta finished for her.

****

"Slow down, Billie," Neeta said for the fourth time in fifteen minutes. "We can't afford to get pulled over."

The car slowed. I stared out the window at familiar landscape. We were close to my home now, close to the city where I'd spent the entirety of my sixteen years. I'd known nothing else except for New Orleans, the city that had left a gaping hole inside my heart.

We were driving north on I-25, through the city of Fountain, Colorado. Through the windshield, I spied the Rocky Mountains looming to the left. The large, dark blue shapes with pine-covered trees washing down the slopes, once a balm to me, now made my blood pressure spike. Rather than think about all the times I hiked in those mountains, the crisp air clearing my lungs, the piney scent of blue spruce clearing my mind, I shut the images, and the feelings that came along with them, out.

I lay across the backseat, my eyes closed so I wouldn't have to see any more, praying that we would make it through the city quickly, without incident, and without a single tear shed.

I hadn't seen my parents in weeks. The last time I'd spoken to my mother, I realized that the woman who'd given birth to me had betrayed me, had tried to have me "brought in". The pain that moment had caused would sit like a stone in my gut quite possibly for the rest of my life. Until that moment, I'd wondered if I'd left prematurely, if I'd judged them unfairly. I hadn't.

With my eyes closed, laying with my head down on the backseat, I could feel the car accelerating again.

Neeta, irritation clear in her voice said, "Billie, slow the hell down."

"I'm trying," I heard Billie say. "I just want to get there."

"We all do, but we'll never get there if we're in jail or worse. If you can't chill, pull over and I'll drive."

Billie sighed, loud and long. "I don't need you to drive. A couple of miles over won't get us in trouble. Don't you think it will look suspicious if we're driving too slow?"

"No, I don't." Neeta's voice was sharp and strong.

The stress of the last few days was getting to everyone. Fuses were short.

We drove in silence for a few more minutes. From what I could tell from my prone position, my eyes still shut tight, we were moving along at a good pace.

I needed to know where we were. "Where are we? What's the nearest exit? Not the number but the street name."

"Woodman Road," Neeta said.

I swallowed bile, again, the french fries threatening to lurch. We were less than ten minutes from my house. The house with the yellow shutters and wide porch, the house with the cobwebby attic where I used to play hide and seek with my aunt, the house with the landscaped front yard where the pulled weeds died in my hand like I was coated in some sort of toxic sludge.

"Billie, there's a cop." Neeta sounded like a robot, her voice low and monotone.

I froze where I was. Popping my head up now would be a mistake.

A half-second later, sirens blared behind us. I'd already been feeling ill. I now felt like I may actually puke, my heartbeat raging inside my chest. A cold sweat broke out under my arms, at the small of my back.

"Fuck," Neeta breathed.

"What do I do?" Billie asked, her voice quaking.

"We have no choice. We have to pull over." Neeta reached a hand back, touching my side. "Sit up but do it slowly and slouch so he doesn't see that you were lying down. Don't forget your seatbelt."

"What do I do?" Billie asked again.

I slowly resumed my seat, keeping my head down as much as possible. I focused on Neeta's hand to keep myself steady and how she gently reached out with it to stroke Billie's arm. "Breathe, pull over, go through the motions, smile, turn on the Billie charm. We're just three ladies on our way to our friend's house." She continued stroking Billie's arm as Billie flipped on the blinker to pull over onto the shoulder.

I looked out the window. I knew the area well. The building to our left, low, with tons of dark windows, had once been a favorite movie theater but was now a storage facility. To our right was a small university, one that had been there forever, and was the kind you could do mostly online. I decided to focus on that building of brick and glass, one I had watched whisk by so many times over the years as I drove by with my family.

The car came to a stop. I had one of those moments where it feels like you're trapped in a nightmare and can't wake up. Dizziness washed over me along with a sickening dread.

Wake up, Miranda.

Only there was no waking up. This was my new reality.

Billie rolled down the window, her finger tapping the steering wheel.

I expected Neeta to chastise our friend over the tapping, but she remained silent. She probably knew, as I did, that the motion was helping Billie to feel grounded in the moment.

After a few minutes, gravel crunched outside the window. The cop was on his way. Billie's hand went dead still, the tapping ceased. There was no longer even the sound of breathing as everyone in the car held their breath.

A shadow loomed to my left. I refused to look, refused to tear my gaze from the university building.

Act like this is no big deal.

"License and registration." A deep voice spoke outside the car.

"Of course," Billie said.

I could hear the smile in her voice, knew without looking that Billie was laying her charm on as thick as she could. Billie was a beautiful woman. When I'd first seen her, I'd thought the statuesque blonde was more suited for the silver screen than walking the streets as a hooker.

We'd never discussed what would happen were we to be pulled over. I had a fake ID, but there'd only been time and funds to procure one for Neeta. She'd remembered an old line cook, Jason, who'd worked in the kitchen at Ruby's, and who'd been busted for making fake IDs a couple of years ago. She'd found the guy living in Baton Rouge, so we'd stopped on the way out of Louisiana. He'd been less than thrilled by Neeta's query, but he still hooked her up with a guy he knew who still made them. We'd gotten lucky. The guy whose name I never got charged us what felt like a fortune for what he said was a *rush job*. Even after saying he'd give us a discount for being a friend of Jason's. After deciding only one of us could get an ID, for the time being, we'd decided on level-headed Neeta who was usually the more in-control of the three of us.

Even though I still had my fake ID, I wasn't sure

if it had been compromised. If Henry had survived the blast in the back alley behind the Fleur de Lis, I was sure the authorities now knew my assumed name. And although I'd had a lot of faith in Trapper, the gruff but kindly proprietor of the Fleur, I wasn't sure how far he would go to protect us.

Whatever the case, Billie had no choice but to give the police officer her actual ID, with her actual name that she loathed above all else.

The cop cleared his throat. "You're a long way from New Orleans. You're Wilhelmina Cowley, but the car is registered to a Crystal Aubert."

Out of the corner of my eye, I saw Neeta lean toward the center console. I felt like I had to burp, but knew if I did, I'd throw up instead.

"Crystal is my mother, Officer. She lent us the car for a little girl's trip."

"I'll need to see your ID then."

"Sure." Neeta fumbled with her wallet. If Neeta decided to give him the fake ID, the names wouldn't match. I couldn't see which one she handed toward the cop's extended hand.

"Seems like a strange time for a trip with everything going on in the world." The officer now had both IDs in his hand with no sign he had any plans to return them, nor did he even gaze down at them.

As this was a statement and not a question, no one replied.

I squeezed my eyes shut, as if that simple action could make all this go away.

"I'll need the three of you to exit the vehicle."

I went ice-cold, a chill wrapping itself around my body until I shivered.

"All of us?" Billie asked.

"All of you." The hulking man backed away from

the car door, his right hand resting on the gun at his hip.

A knot formed in the back of my throat. I was seconds away from panic-crying. Biting down on my lip, I opened the car door, then stepped onto the shoulder of the highway. This stretch was usually busy all times of the day, but this afternoon, there seemed to be hardly anyone about. Maybe because of what was happening, more people were staying indoors. There had been few people on the road the entirety of the trip.

Neeta caught my eye, giving me a little shake of her head. What that shake meant was anyone's guess.

The cop took another step back, a hand still resting on his gun. This was the first time I had seen all of him. He was as big as Trapper, but fitter, and about twenty years younger. He was clean shaven, his eyes hidden behind aviator sunglasses. He was another cliché just like the man I'd seen that morning in Taos, the one whose appearance screamed private detective. "I need the three of you to stand facing the hood of the squad car, hands behind your backs."

Billie huffed a nervous laugh. "But, officer, we weren't going that fast. Is there any other way we can settle this? A ticket, perhaps?" Billie turned toward him, moving a hand up to her hair to twirl a curl.

Without a word, he grabbed her wrist, twisting it behind her as he spun her around to face away from him. As he pulled out cuffs, he said, "There were three girls who caused quite a commotion at a motel in New Orleans. The girls haven't been seen since, but it was believed they slipped town. Oddly, the three of you match the descriptions. Do not fight me or I will use deadly force."

Frozen to my spot, my hands clasped behind my back, I shot a look at Neeta who was gazing dead ahead, then over at Billie whose face had gone beet red. Tears fell from Billie's eyes, her head shaking back and forth. "Do what you have to," she said, a microsecond before turning around.

She whirled so fast the cop dropped the cuffs to the concrete with a clatter. His hand darted to his gun. I heard the click of the gun being unsecured from his belt as I too, whirled around.

With one blast of blue light from the palm of Billie's hand, the man flew backward, slamming into the rear of Crystal's SUV. He crumpled forward, sliding down the back and onto the cement in a heap.

All I could think of was Henry. He looked much the same when I blasted him with my blue light, slamming him into the back wall of the Fleur and tumbling him into a similar pile of arms and legs.

Neeta ran over to the police officer, carefully reaching out a hand to check for a pulse.

I pulled Billie close to me as I looked behind us for cars. There was no one.

Billie shook in my arms.

"He's alive. I think he'll live, probably just a concussion," Neeta said. "We need to move him into his car fast, then get the hell out of here."

She looked toward me and Billie, both of us still frozen on the side of the road. "Now," she barked with enough force to snap us out of our dazes.

Billie darted forward to take the man's legs. Neeta and I each took an arm, and together the three of us half-carried, half-drug the muscular police officer to the side door of his vehicle. We shoved him in the best we could, running back to the SUV to jump in and speed off.

Just as we pulled back out into the road, two cars sped by.

"If he ran the plates, we're fucked." Neeta, still in the passenger seat, held her upper arms as if she could hug the nightmare away.

Billie was slumped in the back.

I was in the driver's seat. I'd insisted I drive now, being the most familiar with the area.

"I know," I said as I flicked on the blinker. "At the very least, he'll have the description once he wakes up. That's why this car is dead to us."

"Where are you going?" Billie breathed from the back seat.

I glanced at her through the rearview, shocked at the sheer whiteness of my friend's complexion. A blue vein throbbed in Billie's forehead.

"Home."

"Are you crazy?" Neeta reached out like she may grab the steering wheel, then thought better of it, pulling her hand back into her lap. "You can't go to your house. Are you forgetting what your parents did to you?"

I did my best not to stare daggers at Neeta. "No, I'll never forget what they did. But what choice do we have? My dad will be at work. If Mom is home alone, maybe I can reason with her. Maybe if she sees me in the flesh, puts her arms around me, she'll take some sort of mercy on us." I shook my head. "I can't think of anything else to do. I don't know anyone else who would possibly help us, and we can't steal a car. We're not exactly seasoned criminals. How far do you think we'd get? They'd really shoot us on sight if we did that."

"Miranda's right." Billie clicked in her seatbelt, her voice steadier. "It's a calculated risk. However, I'm not above stealing a car if we have to. At this point, we don't have much to lose. We're wanted by the authorities any way you look at it, and now we know for sure. I say plan A is to feel out her mom, plan B is to get the hell out of there and boost the first car we find."

"Boost?" Neeta craned her neck to look back at

Billie. "What do you know about boosting anything?"

"I've been operating outside the law for years, obviously. I may not know how to do it, but I know the lingo."

Neeta snorted a laugh. "Okay, babe. Plan B is we boost a car."

Chapter Three

The street I'd lived on almost my entire life seemed foreign to me as I tapped the brakes, rolling slowly toward my house.

It was the middle of the day. The chances of someone seeing us were pretty good. Neeta had offered to drive, but I knew it had to be me. I had to grip the steering wheel in both hands, eyes on the manicured lawns. Each house was a replica of the one next to it, each two stories with small porches and big front windows. Lawns were green, even during yet another drought, and colorful flowers lined walkways.

The door to my two-car garage was open, the trunk of my mom's sedan, sitting in one of the bays, popped open, bags of groceries visible within. The other bay, the one designated for Dad's truck, was empty.

I took a full breath. Although my dad had never done me any harm, I'd always been closer to my mom, always felt, until the betrayal, that Mom had always been on my side. My hope was simple. I hoped that once my mom saw me in the flesh, with her own motherly eyes, that maybe, just maybe, she'd feel compelled to help. How cold would one person have to be to have lost all feeling for their child?

"I can't believe we're doing this." Neeta sucked in a breath as I turned the car into the driveway.

"We must be desperate," Billie breathed, leaning forward so far, her breath tickled my ear. "We're driving right into the belly of the beast."

I pulled Crystal's SUV behind the beige four-door, my heart thumping in my throat.

Is that even possible?

"The only thing that has any color around here is

the grass." Neeta eyed her surroundings, a finger tapping the door handle. "You never would have bloomed here, magic or not. The mountains are beautiful, though, and the air is probably the freshest I've ever smelled, but these people need an injection of life."

"I think I've had a little too much life. If I could go back to the days of staring at the peeling walls of the Fleur de Lis, I probably would." Billie adjusted her seat, dipping lower to look out the windshield.

I put the car in park but left it running, my hand tight on the gear shift. "Yeah, I would too, only don't judge the Springs by this one neighborhood. Downtown is awesome. You guys would love the old buildings, the shops, the much more liberal vibe. Life is more colorful there."

As I stared ahead, into the dim void of the garage, the door opened, my mother stepping down alongside her car.

I almost bit through my lip. There was Mom, dark hair pulled back in a ponytail, sunglasses perched on the top of her head, dressed in her usual uniform of tan slacks with a muted, thin sweater, even though it was late summer, the temperature soaring.

There was an unwritten parental rule, a rule that moms were always supposed to love and protect their children no matter what. No matter what they'd done or said, a mom was always supposed to stand in front of you, protecting you, pushing you out of harm's way.

On TV, I had seen moms of murderers sit behind their children in court, not supporting what their child had done, but just being there. I hadn't hurt anyone. Except for Henry and that was self-defense. What had happened to me had not been my fault. Had I been given a choice, I would not have wanted the magic; I would have rejected it. Still, my mother had not supported me, had not helped me, had only tried to set me up so that I could be taken in by the authorities.

"This was a mistake."

My mother looked up as she walked toward the front of the garage. She cocked her head to the side, her eyes squinting to get a better look at who sat behind the darkened glass of the SUV. Her hand reached out, her palm resting on the side of her car as realization dawned in her eyes.

Without looking away from me, she shut the still open trunk, groceries that would go bad in the heat within, then took one tentative step onto the driveway.

I didn't back away. I just kept my eyes locked with those of my mother.

Billie gripped my headrest, her breath loud in my ear.

Neeta reached over a hand, her own eyes locked on the woman in front of us. She wrapped her fingers around my wrist, her touch light but hot.

"What are we doing?" Billie whispered. "Are we going?"

"You two, stay in the car." I opened the door, my heart skipping beats in my chest. My hands were clammy, slipping off the door as I tried pushing it open farther.

Neeta relinquished her hold of my wrist, Billie making some sort of grunting sound.

I stepped out, my mother not more than five feet away, a look of shock on her face.

For a second, we just stood there, me on the pavement, shielded by the car door, my mother in front of the SUV's rounded hood.

Mom's throat bobbed with a swallow. "What are you doing here?"

This wasn't the question I wanted to hear. I'd

hoped to hear something more akin to, *How can I help you?,* but I already knew I hoped for too much. The disappointment welled deep within, my chest deflating with a long exhale. My throat burned, but I refused to cry, refused even to let my eyes swim.

"We're in trouble. If we don't get off the streets, hide this car, we're done for. Who knows where we'll be taken or what will happen to us." My voice sounded alien to me, less childlike, deeper almost, as if in the last five minutes I'd matured about ten years. There was no time to go into specifics. Every second that passed put us more firmly in danger.

My mother's eyes flicked to the passengers inside the car, her head again dipping to the side. A crease formed between her brows. "Who's with you?"

"Friends. Women like me who have changed against their will." I gripped the inside of the door handle with wet hands, ready to jump back into the car and speed away in one last desperate attempt to evade the law.

Mom scrutinized Neeta and Billie through the glass. "Pull the car into the garage."

I sensed the shock registering across my face. "What?"

Mom glanced around, up and down the street. "Do it quickly, although it may already be too late." She dug into the pocket of her colorless pants, pulling out a jangle of keys. She tossed these at me, over the door I still hid behind. "Your dad is out of town. He returns in two days. Tomorrow I'll report my car stolen, so you'll have at least 24 hours."

I caught the keys in one hand, my mouth gaping open.

Neeta hissed from the passenger seat. "How can we trust her? She already screwed you over once."

Mom stared through the windshield at Neeta, her

eyes as blank as her face. "And I regret that. This is my opportunity to wipe the slate clean, to atone for betraying my daughter. There's food in the trunk, and about sixty in cash in the console. I'll take this car and leave it somewhere. I can't do any more. I wish I could, but I can't."

"Grab your stuff," I said to Neeta and Billie, my gaze still glued to Mom. This was it, our only option to evade the law and make it to my aunt in Estes Park. Mom was right, it may already be too late. The choice was to act now, or risk being seen.

Could my mother call the cops the second we pulled away in her car? Yes, yes, she could, but if we stayed in Crystal's car, the car that had been pulled over and was now on the police's radar, we were done for. Going with my mother's plan was the only plan. There was a fifty-fifty chance Mom would buy us the time we needed. We had no other chance if we didn't take her up on her offer.

"Are you insane?" Neeta grabbed her backpack as she asked this question. Not wanting to abandon Crystal's car, unsure if we could trust my mom, but also knowing options were limited.

Billie grabbed up her stuff from the backseat as she popped open the back door. "I think we all passed insane some time ago. We're on our way to batshit."

I had yet to move from where I stood as around me, Billie and Neeta jumped into action.

Neeta gave my mom a wide berth as she made her way to the passenger side of the beige sedan, opening the door and throwing in her belongings.

Billie followed suit, also throwing her things into the back seat as the trunk had been full of groceries.

"Miranda, pop the back."

Still in a trance, I leaned down and pressed the

button that opened the back of Crystal's SUV. Billie grabbed out my suitcase and quilt, trotting back to the sedan to throw these items in with everything else.

As Billie walked with her long stride past my mother, Mom's gaze fell on the quilt.

"I thought you must have taken it with you. I'm glad." She said this almost more to herself than to me.

"I needed something from home, something to tether me to my roots, or so I thought."

Mom blinked several times, which made me think maybe she was blinking away tears, but not a drop fell from her eyes.

Billie shoved the suitcase and quilt onto the backseat, then stood there, Neeta just behind her, both of them laser focused on me.

I closed the door of Crystal's SUV. A deep breath caused painful nausea to bubble in my stomach. I stepped toward my mom. I wasn't sure what I expected, I surely didn't expect a hug, not after everything that had happened, but when my mom took a step away from me, all the air seemed to whoosh from my lungs in one exhale.

She was afraid of me.

Mom watched me with a wary eye, one foot braced behind like she may try to turn and flee, while I held out the keys for the SUV.

When mom didn't so much as hold out her hand, I dropped the keys with a clang on the pavement of the driveway. The keys rested half on an oil stain that had been there since I was little. I used to draw a yellow ring around that round stain, making it the sun in chalk drawings when I was still too young for school.

Mom, in her gingham shorts, would weed the garden while little me drew pictures all over the driveway, watching the kids walk home from the nearby elementary school.

One day, Mom called me over to where she was crouched near the roses, a wide smile spread on her face to show me a tiny family of ladybugs making their home within the petals of the blush pink flowers. She'd rubbed my back with love and affection while I cupped my hand around the rose, careful not to hurt the ladybugs, but just wanting to watch a little closer.

Now, my mom couldn't even stand to brush my fingertips to exchange a key ring. I'd become a foreign object to my mother, something other, something unknown.

I was sure I felt something die within me. Maybe it was hope. Hope that Mom and I would ever move past this, would ever be what we once were.

Pain spasmed in my chest as my throat tightened. My eyes burned. The telltale warmth spread in the palms of my hands, and I knew if I didn't get myself under control, my mom may have even more cause to be afraid.

I squeezed my hands closed tight, willing myself to take deep breaths. I wanted more than anything to be able to feel my emotions without the magic rising up, unbidden.

"Time to get the hell out of here, honey." Neeta wrapped me in a pair of strong, warm arms. She tugged me to the side and then forward. "I think I'll drive us the rest of the way." She walked me over to the open passenger door, kissed me on the top of my head, then gently shoved me down onto the seat. Neeta reached in, buckling my belt, then slammed the door.

The car smelled like Mom. The old-fashioned floral perfume she always wore surrounded me, assailing my senses with a flood of memories I didn't want. I'd remembered enough. Closing my eyes against the onslaught of remembrances, I leaned my head back against the headrest.

Billie got into the back, a tight squeeze with all our belongings packed in. She reached an arm up to give me an awkward from-behind hug. "We got you, honey. Cry if you need to. It's okay. I'm going to." Billie's voice cracked on the last word.

Neeta slid into the driver's seat, her gaze on the rearview mirror.

The car behind us, the comfortable SUV that Crystal had so generously given us to run in, roared to life. I opened my eyes, staring straight ahead. From my peripheral vision, I saw the SUV glide into the empty garage bay next to us.

Don't turn your head.

It took every ounce of willpower I possessed to not turn my fixed gaze upon my mother.

The coldness in Mom's eyes had been what had shocked me the most, the utter lack of emotion. Had I changed so much in just a few short weeks that I now felt like a stranger to my own mother? I willed the pain in my heart away. I had to. I had to go numb to cease the sadness, the disappointment, the heartache. Those feelings wouldn't serve me now. Maybe I could revisit them at another time, a time in the future when I was safe. Safe to allow the emotions to flow through me, identifying and dealing with each one in turn.

Without wasting any more time, Neeta pulled out, out of the garage where I played darts with my dad, over the driveway I filled with colorful chalk drawings, past the garden tended with my mom, past the house I'd spent all my life.

"Miranda." Neeta gripped the steering wheel in both hands, her knuckles blanched from the effort, like she was holding on for dear life. "How the hell do I get out of this wonderbread neighborhood? Do these people realize that every house looks exactly the damn same?"

"Neeta don't be so grumpy. Miranda just went through something awful." Billie released me to settle into the back seat.

"That's why I'm grumpy, Bill."

I held up a limp hand, pointing the way ahead. "Turn left up ahead, then you'll go straight until you see the signs for the interstate. We're not far from being back on our way."

"Good. The sooner we get to this Estes Park place, the better."

****

"Miranda, wake up." The strong hand of Neeta gripped my thigh, giving my leg a light shove.

I groaned, my neck aching from sleeping in such an uncomfortable position, my head throbbing with exhaustion and what was likely dehydration. Once we were back on the road—Neeta understanding where we were going from there—I, my limbs feeling like leaden weights, had lain the seat back, lolled my head to the side, and fell into a dreamless sleep.

I rubbed the crust from my eyes, blinking away the bleariness as I took in where we were.

Pine trees loomed all around, limbs appearing like living things in the darkening sky. The luscious curve of the Rocky Mountains appeared like a jagged rollercoaster ahead. We were driving west, straight for the spectacular range.

"We can't be here already." My tongue felt heavy. I longed for a toothbrush and a glass of water.

"We are. That freaky hotel is up there, the next right."

Although expensive, we'd agreed to stay the night at the Stanley Hotel. This was the location I was sure Aunt Bea had directed me to. The only question was, how long would it take my aunt to find us? If it took longer than a few nights, we'd be out of money and out of options.

We turned onto the drive for the Stanley Hotel. The hotel was huge, white with a red roof. Two long wings placed at each end of the building seemed to reach out to us like arms. After all we'd been through, the effect was creepy rather than welcoming. The sky over the hotel was blue swirled with pink and orange from the setting sun. Billowing white clouds floated through these bright colors, the whole thing looking like a mixed bag of cotton candy.

I heard Billie whisper, *Cool,* from the backseat. It might have been cool if not for the fact that we were wanted women, running from everything we'd ever known.

"What's your aunt's name, again?" Neeta turned the steering wheel as she slowed down, maneuvering through the parking lot.

"Beatrice, Aunt Bea."

"What does she look like, Miranda? In case one of us sees her and you're not around." Billie had unbuckled her seatbelt and was gathering up loose items to shove into her pink bag.

"She doesn't look like my mom at all. In fact, she used to crack jokes all the time about being adopted. Just wishful thinking, I guess." I took a breath as I thought about my aunt's physical characteristics. "She's tall, like six feet. Her hair is wiry, orangey. She always called herself a redhead, but really her natural color is more orange, like a tabby cat. Pale skin, like Billie, not darker olive like my mom's. Freckles like you wouldn't believe all over her face, chest, arms. The only resemblance between us is our eyes, hers are brown, too. If she still dresses the same, she'll stand out a bit. My dad used to call her a hippie, and I guess if this were the 80s, people would still call her that. She wears sandals and flowy dresses, scarves, and crystal necklaces. That kind of stuff."

Neeta huffed a laugh. "She sounds like what my mom would call a character. Which is what I consider all my favorite people to be, so I like her already."

"There's no room for boring around here," Billie agreed.

"I think we passed boring about three weeks ago." I cackled a laugh at my own joke. Even though I'd slept the last few hours, I still felt more tired than I ever had in my life, slap happy almost.

Billie snorted in the backseat, Neeta chuckling as she pulled into a parking spot.

Chapter Four

The lobby was expansive with gleaming, dark wood floors. A few nicely dressed people walked by us, making me feel self-conscious about my rumpled tank top and jeans, and the way I was sure I looked in general.

A glance to the side told me Billie and Neeta likely had the same misgivings. Billie tucked a stray curl behind her ear, her gaze finding the floor, and Neeta shuffled her feet, her backpack clutched in front of her like a shield. "Let's get this over with," she mumbled, tightening her grip on her bag as she moved toward the registration desk.

I realized two things in rapid succession. One, Neeta was going to be testing her new fake ID for the first time. She'd given her real one to the cop.

The second concern was whether we'd be able to rent a room with cash only. No one could risk using a credit card. We had to be as untraceable as possible. This hadn't been a problem in Taos. That place had no issues dealing in cash, but this hotel would probably require a credit card for incidentals.

Neeta stopped in her tracks. I nearly tripped over my feet as she came to an abrupt stop.

She whirled on us. "I just thought of something." She made a face as if disgusted with herself. "There is obviously some sort of APB out on the three of us after the stunt at the Fleur de lis." Neeta's head turned from side to side, taking in the scene around us.

"What should we do, then?" I was tired, and my skin felt like an oil slick. All I wanted was a room with a nice bed, a hot shower, and a change of clothes.

"You two go back out to the car." Neeta adjusted her ballcap, winding up her braids to stuff underneath.

"I'll do my best to get the room, then come and get you."

Billie shook her head so vehemently she looked like a toddler about to have a tantrum. "No way. We agreed, or maybe we didn't, but we should have. The three of us stick together, at all times, no matter what."

"Billie's right, Neeta. We can't help you if we're in the parking lot and something goes wrong. I know we would both be more comfortable with you in our sights."

Neeta shouldered her backpack, her eyebrows set in a way that I knew meant she was determined. "Too much of a chance we'll be recognized. I'll be fine. This should be a breeze compared to being pulled over." She leveled Billie with a stare. "Besides, I'll be able to sell my story better if I'm alone."

I sighed, shooting a sideways glance at Billie.

Billie met my gaze, giving me a slight nod. "Okay." She reached out a hand to take Neeta by the arm. "If you feel like things are in any way going south, or the person seems shifty, just fucking split. I'll have the car running."

Neeta nodded, her lips pursed in what would have seemed like determination, had it not been for the slight quiver.

I caught Billie's slender hand, pulling her away, out the door of the main lobby. We walked back to the car as fast as we could without trying to make it too obvious we were in a hurry.

Billie got into the driver's seat. "I hate this. I hate every second of this. I just want my life back, shitty though it was."

I slumped in the passenger seat, my stare fixed on the main doors of the hotel. "We're going to get through this. We have to." I turned to Billie. "This might be stupid, but what if we, like, channeled all our positive thoughts and feelings toward Neeta? I mean, we're something like witches, aren't we? Let's start actually thinking like witches."

Billie nodded. "Okay, I like this idea. Let's do it."

She held up her hand, *Thelma and Louise* style for me to grasp. Then, we turned our attention to our friend who at that moment needed all the magic she could get.

I took deep breaths, visualizing Neeta while I did so.

Give Neeta a room. Give Neeta a room.

I chanted this over and over to myself as I visualized Neeta walking up to the counter, smiling at a nice lady with a nametag that read *Sara*, and asking politely, in her sweetest, southern voice with her brightest smile for a room.

I slipped into a trance as I stared ahead. Sara was nodding yes and asking for a credit card to hold the room. To this, Neeta would respond that it was vital she pay in cash. Her no-good ex was violent, and he was after her. She was trying to get to her mother, and the only way she'd be able to do that was if *he* was unable to trace the card from their mutual account. Would the kind lady please consider taking cash? She could pay for the room in full and shouldn't need to stay for longer than two nights.

Sara's face changed. Sara nodded solemnly like she understood on another level what Neeta was requesting. *This isn't something we do often,* Sara was saying, *but we do occasionally make exceptions for this very reason.*

I can't thank you enough, Neeta said back.

Two minutes later and Neeta held a key card in her hand. She thanked Sara again as she backtracked out the lobby doors.

Billie squeezed my hand. "Did you see all that?"

"The clerk named Sara?"

Billie dropped my hand, a look of pure fright in her eyes. "Yeah."

I nodded.

The back door opened, startling us so badly we yelped in unison.

"Get your stuff, bitches. We got ourselves a room."

****

The room was small. One double bed sat in the center of the room, the headboard against the left wall. A small couch sat beneath a window overlooking the east side of the property. One of us would have to sleep on it, and I was happy for it to be me. Billie kicked in her sleep and Neeta snored, although both would deny this until the end of their days.

I crossed the short distance to the sofa, tossed my stuff on it, and took off for the bathroom. "Dibs on the first shower."

Billie dove on the bed while Neeta ambled up alongside the couch to peek out the curtains.

Billie kicked off her shoes, each one landing with a soft thud on the tan carpet. "A quick call to Joey wouldn't hurt anything, would it? He did give me a number to a burner phone before he left."

I stopped at the door of the bathroom, a hand braced on the wood frame. Neeta made a sound of disgust, pinning me in a wide-eyed stare. "Billie, I know we've been through a lot, but have you lost all sense? If you don't think Joey is being surveilled, you know absolutely nothing about how the world works. Burner phone or not, we all agreed, no contact with anyone outside of Miranda's aunt. We kind of blew that with her mom, but we didn't have a choice. I just don't trust anything."

Billie rolled onto her back, staring up at the

ceiling. "I don't see how a two-minute phone call to a burner phone, just to check in, just to let him know I'm alive and okay, would be such a big deal. They can't trace a call in two-minutes, can they?"

"Yes, I'm sure *they* can," Neeta emphasized the word they.

The thing is none of us knew exactly who *they* were. The three of us had lumped all government and law enforcement agencies into one all-encompassing category. Which organization was at the head of the snake was not something we'd taken much time to consider. Not that it really mattered. To us, *they* could be the FBI, the CIA, or even some other agency we'd never even heard of. I imagined it was some new organization, maybe put together by someone as powerful as the president, created solely to deal with the problem of the witches, as we were being called on every news outlet.

"The fact is," Neeta continued, her back now to the closed window. "We don't know a damn thing about who could be out there hunting us. We have to be smart, not only to protect ourselves, but our loved ones as well. We all have people we want to call."

"I don't," I said without thinking. I bit into my lip as I leaned against the door frame.

"Of course you do, Miranda. You have Ash." Billie spoke softly, her gaze still on the ceiling. "I know she means as much to you as Joey means to me."

The last thing I wanted to do was feel more pain. I squeezed my eyes shut as I bit down harder on my lip. I bit until I tasted blood. Physical pain was a hundred times better than the ache in my heart, in my soul, the almost near constant pressure in the back of my throat that meant one thing, I could cry at the drop of a hat.

I opened my eyes, a hard swallow nearly choking me. "After the two of you, and Aunt Bea, she means more to me than anyone on earth. Which is why I can't call her, which is why I can never call her, and why I will probably never see her again. You need to set your mind to these facts, Bill. This is where we are now. We're outcasts, outlaws. We can never go back."

Billie's head rolled toward me. Tears stood in my friends' eyes, sitting on her lashes like dew on blades of grass. Billie didn't say a word. She rolled until she was on her stomach, her face pressed into the pillow. Her back heaved with what I knew were sobs.

I wanted to comfort her but was so close to breaking myself that all I could do was throw a blank stare at Neeta then retreat into the cool interior of the all-white bathroom.

I closed the door behind me, slumping against it. There had been few occasions to be alone in the last couple of days, and I relished this moment. I'd been harsh with Billie. My intention hadn't been to sound so cold, so mean, but what would it serve us to hold on to the past? There was only pain in holding on.

Beyond the door, bedsprings creaked. I imagined Neeta kneeling on the bed next to our friend, rubbing her back until she felt better.

I propelled myself forward. I gripped the edge of the sink, staring at my reflection in the mirror. A stranger stared back. I knew I was an attractive person. I'd been told so all my life. The last year I'd grown into my body, filling out in the places a young woman is supposed to. My chestnut hair, always full and bouncy, had once been a source of pride. My smooth skin had only rarely been marred by a hormonal teenage pimple, and my vintage style had always been unique.

Now, I appeared a ghost of the girl I was only weeks, even days, ago. My skin had lost its healthy sheen and now appeared sallow. My cheeks were almost sunken. My dark eyes, usually bright, were dim and dull. The hair I usually styled so carefully hung limp around my shoulders as I pulled it from the band holding it back.

I closed my eyes, resting my forehead against the mirror. The coolness felt good.

Unbidden thoughts of Ash sprung to mind. I knew this was something I would never escape. All I could hope for was that time would diminish these thoughts, the memories of a short time in my life when I'd been more myself than I'd ever been before.

I thought of our date at the movie theater, seeing an old, throwback movie called *Trainspotting*. Me and Ash had been the only people in the midnight showing of the film and had taken full advantage of the empty theater by acting out a silly little scene. We'd been just getting to know each other, and we'd laughed and smiled so much that my cheeks were sore by the end of the movie. The scene changed in my mind, and we were now on another date. Ash had brought me a bright bouquet of sunflowers for our picnic at City Park. I took a deep breath as if I could still smell the sunshine baked into the yellow petals.

Before I could get much farther in this memory, a knock sounded on a door.

My heart stopped. I held my breath and listened. Had someone just knocked on the door to our hotel room?

I opened the bathroom door a crack, peeping through the space.

In the room, Neeta stood rigid near the foot of the bed as she stared at the door.

Billie half-sat, half-leaned on the bed, her attention also on the room door.

I opened the bathroom door the rest of the way, taking one quiet step forward. "Who is it?" I mouthed at

Neeta.

Neeta shrugged with a shake of her head. My friend's eyes were as big as the moon, her chest heaving in much the same way mine was.

I knew the onus was on me to find out. I passed a hand over my stomach, churning with nausea, as I crept forward on my tiptoes. No matter that the floor was carpeted, I couldn't risk even the slightest creak of a floorboard underneath.

Before I was halfway there, a soft voice called through the door, "Flower, open up."

I wanted to sink to my knees, and almost did when my knees gave out one then the other. Instead of falling, I braced a hand on the wall, and continued on. I grabbed the knob, wrenching it to the side and throwing open the door.

There stood Aunt Bea in all her tie-dyed glory.

I walked into my aunt's arms, inhaling lavender.

"Did you check the peephole before you opened the door?"

"No," I said as I held my aunt tight, half in the doorway, half in the hall. "You said Flower. Who else would know to call me that?"

"Anyone who's been opening my correspondence." She rubbed my back in circles like my mom used to do. "But I'm just so darn happy to see you that I'll let it go."

Warmth spread through me at this contact with my aunt. I hadn't been held like this by a family member in some time, and I wanted to relish this moment.

Aunt Bea gave me a gentle push back. "Let's get out of the hall and behind a closed and locked door."

We stepped into the room, Aunt Bea closing the door behind her with a thud. My aunt looked good, a bit skinny maybe, but healthy and strong. She wore a pink and white tie-dyed dress that brushed the tops of her feet, exposing brown sandals that had seen better days. Her long, wiry orange hair was tied back with a white scarf and slung over one shoulder she toted a large black cotton bag. I spied shapely muscles in her exposed arms and wondered if she'd been working out.

She looked me up and down. A smile bloomed across her freckled cheeks. "It's been too long, kiddo. Way too long. You look good, Mira. You've become a woman."

I felt my face go red, warmth spreading over my chest and neck. "Auntie." I dipped my head, my arms crossing in front of me.

"Oh, stop that, Mira." Aunt Bea reached out her index finger, tipping my chin up. "Hold that head up high."

"Kind of hard to do when we're in hiding." Neeta's voice had an edge to it that I understood.

"Well." Aunt Bea beamed her smile in Neeta's direction. "That's true enough, isn't it? But things won't always be like this."

"I wish I had your confidence," Neeta retorted.

"Neeta," Billie chided, still in her strange half-crouched position on the bed. "Don't be rude to Miranda's aunt."

"I don't detect any rudeness, only truths." Aunt Bea stuck out a hand as she moved toward Neeta. "Neeta, is it? I'm Aunt Bea, or Bea, or Auntie. Just please don't call me Beatrice."

I watched as Neeta took my aunt's hand, gently pumping it up and down. My friend's face softened. "Nice to meet you. I'm sure I speak for everyone when I say we're relieved down to the ground that you found us."

"I'm Billie. I hate my full name, too." Billie slid

off the end of the bed, as tall as my aunt when she was standing straight up. She too held out a hand which Aunt Bea took. "How did you find us, by the way?"

Hands dropped. Aunt Bea made her way over to the couch, sitting down as she said, "First of all, I'm pleased to meet you both. I can't thank you enough for banding together with my Flower. We're stronger together. It's when we're alone, isolated, that they get us. As for how I found you, the lady who checked you in—Sara—she's one of us."

Neeta sat on the edge of the bed, Billie sitting alongside her. Neeta nodded. "I thought there was some kind of recognition in her eyes. I thought maybe she'd been a victim of abuse, but she has the powers, as we do."

"Like most of us, she's both a victim of abuse, and a witch." Aunt Bea pulled her large black bag onto the couch with her.

"Is that what we are?" I perched on the arm of the couch, hovering over her and the rest of the room.

"Yes, that's what we are. What else would we be, Mira?" Aunt Bea craned her neck to look up.

I shrugged. "We've been avoiding that word because it's just so, so…" I swallowed. "Weird."

Aunt Bea laughed. I missed that laugh, more of a masculine chuckle. "This is definitely weird. But there isn't another word that so encompasses what we are, what we can do. We can wield magic with our bodies and with our minds. We can manipulate energy, work spells, create potions. Each of us has our own gifts. There is overlap in the power, but some of us are better at certain things than others."

Billie's eyes went wide, her jaw dropping open for a second. "Spells, potions? How do you know all this?"

"I know." Aunt Bea turned her attention to Billie. "Because I've spent the last couple of years traveling, learning all I can from every witch I've come across. I've amassed quite a lot on the subject. I didn't think the world would explode the way it did, so it's lucky for all of us that I did the legwork." She stuck her hand in her black bag, pulling forth a huge, brown leather book. The pages inside were crinkled, weathered, some of them poking out like they weren't bound. The book was wrapped with a leather cord the same color as the cover. "This, my dears, is my grimoire."

Neeta narrowed her eyes, her gaze on the strange book. "Your what?"

"My grimoire. These pages hold accounts of everything I've experienced over the last two years, not to mention every spell and potion I've learned of. Inside this book is everything the three of you need to know to control your magic, strengthen your magic, and develop as witches."

Billie bit her bottom lip, a smile splitting her face. She shot Neeta a look, then me. "This is everything we were hoping for," she breathed. "Suddenly, I feel a hundred times lighter."

I wanted to feel the same. I was certainly relieved to be with my aunt. For all my bravado of being on my own for the past several weeks, there was a certain relaxation in knowing there was someone to care for me now. But the lightness Billie confessed to feeling did not manifest in me. Oddly, there was a heaviness, more responsibility that I didn't want. There was more to learn, more to control, more that would make me different.

When both myself and Neeta had remained silent, Billie looked at each of us in turn. "You guys, this is great. Don't you think this is great? Isn't this what we wanted?"

"This is what we wanted," Neeta agreed. "It's just a lot."

"Neeta's correct, this is more than a lot. You dears have already been through so much, and I'm afraid life won't be getting much easier. If anything, there is more for you to do now."

"But we're safe. With you." Billie looked at Aunt Bea, a plea for refuge in her eyes.

"You're as safe with me as I am with me," Aunt Bea said simply.

"What does that mean?" Distress was entering Billie's voice.

Neeta reached out a hand to hold Billie's.

"What it means," I said as I sank onto the couch next to my aunt, "is that we'll never be safe. Not really. Not until we're no longer considered a threat."

Aunt Bea nodded her head in agreement. "Until we're no longer a threat or until we come to some sort of understanding with the government."

"How could we come to an understanding with them? They're terrified of us." I was staring off into space, trying desperately not to feel the burden of all that was to come.

"Yes, and we'll use that fear to our advantage by freeing the women who've been taken. When we're all together, as one force, the government will have to listen to us."

It was Neeta's turn to laugh. "Free the women?"

"All of them?" Billie shrieked.

Aunt Bea's face remained placid, a pleasant half-smile on her lips. "As many as we can. I've been making a list. Like I told Miranda in my letter, there aren't as many of us as the media is making out. It's all hysteria, really. You'd think there were hundreds, wouldn't you? Maybe even thousands, but in reality, witches are rare.

There are probably less than fifty in all of the United States, and as far as I've been able to tell, there are less than that in custody."

"So, what you're saying is it's a miracle the three of us found each other." Neeta was chewing on her lip.

"Not a miracle. We're attracted to each other's energy. This is how I've been able to find others of our kind on my travels. I can pinpoint them relatively easily. You'll learn to do the same in a conscious way." Aunt Bea stuffed her grimoire back inside her bag.

"What if we don't want to put ourselves at such risk? We have people, people who would like to see us alive one day." Neeta's face registered pain as she said this. She crossed her legs, shifting her gaze to the ground.

"Whether you wish to help me free our sisters is entirely up to each of you. I can't force you, nor do I wish to. I'll teach you regardless, but my hope is that you will choose to do what is right. The right move is to help these women, to band together, to force them to take us seriously and to stop putting us away." Aunt Bea rose to her feet, slinging her bag over a shoulder. "Take the night to relax and think through your decisions. You have the room. You may as well use it."

She turned to open her arms to me, and I stood for a hug. "My place isn't far from here. I'll be back in the morning. We can have a nice breakfast and talk some more."

"We have to get rid of the car. It's Mom's." I blurted this into Aunt Bea's ear. "She said she'd report it stolen by tomorrow afternoon."

Aunt Bea held on to my arms, pulling back from the hug to stare into my eyes. "What? You've seen her?"

I nodded. I was beginning to feel as if I was operating in some sort of brain fog, like I'd had the flu and wasn't recovering so well.

"You're nodding, but you're not explaining, Mira. What happened with your mom? Actually, come to think of it, you never told me why you ran in the first place." Aunt Bea continued to gently hold my arms, looking me in the face while she spoke.

"I'm not sure what there is to explain." I pulled myself loose, leaning a hip against the arm of the couch. "I ran because the power was starting to make its presence known. There were news stories one after the next, so many that I panicked. Mom and Dad both began acting weird around me, whispering in hallways, sliding sideways glances at each other. I freaked, and I ran. And it was a good thing I did, because once I tried to call them from New Orleans, there was someone at the house, someone who was trying to get my mom to find out where I was."

"Oh, my god." Aunt Bea clamped a hand over her mouth, then moved it up to grab onto a loose curl. "I can't believe they betrayed you like that. Their only daughter. I'm so ashamed of my sister I could spit. But that's our upbringing for you. Our upbringing and your dad's influence. So, how did you end up with her car?"

Neeta stirred on the bed. "My mom gave us her SUV to leave New Orleans in, but we got pulled over in Colorado Springs. One of us" —Neeta inclined her head toward Billie— "may have blasted the cop who pulled us over. So, out of options, we went to Miranda's. Her mom was there. It was tense, let me tell you, but she ended up giving us the keys to her sedan. She said once her husband returns tomorrow, she'd report the car as stolen."

"Bitch," Aunt Bea muttered. "Well, at least she helped you in a dire moment." She held a hand out to me. "Give me the keys. I'll take the car and dispose of it."

"Dispose of it, how?" I fished the keys from my pocket.

Aunt Bea shrugged. "I'll figure it out. Sara will help me. Don't worry about it. What I want you three to do now is order some room service, sleep, and talk about what I've proposed. The car is nothing more than a minor inconvenience."

Chapter Five

Two hours after Aunt Bea left, I was showered, my belly was full, and I was drowsily lounging on the couch I would call my bed for the night.

The sky beyond the window was dark, the clear sky filled with a million twinkling stars.

Neeta and Billie sat on the double bed, backs against the headboard. Billie was tucked in the blankets, face washed, teeth brushed, ready for sleep, while Neeta's feet, kicked free of the covers, twitched with energy like she could get up and dance around the room.

Neeta had turned down the temperature so far that I shivered under my thin, spare blanket. I had changed into pajama pants, a sweatshirt over the tank top I'd worn all day. Clothes had to be worn sparingly. I had no idea when I'd be able to wash them again. There was no telling what sort of facilities Aunt Bea had at her place.

"We've successfully avoided the topic for a couple of hours. I'm opening the floor." Neeta flourished her hands in front of her in dramatic fashion.

"Whatever that means." Billie slid farther under the covers, yanking them up under her chin. "Could you lower the thermostat any more, Neeta? I feel like I'm in the Arctic Circle."

"I'm anxious, okay? And when I get anxious, I get hot." She fanned her face with an open hand to make her point. "We can call for more blankets."

"No way." I shook my head, cradled in the small pillow. "Talk about anxious, I was nervous enough calling for room service."

"Miranda's right, and I'm surprised you're the one suggesting such a thing. We don't need to make ourselves too conspicuous." Billie tucked the blanket under her chin. "Since you're the one who opened the floor, or whatever, you start."

"Fine, I will. Of course, we're going to help Bea, right? I mean, what else would we do? We can't let other women, women like us, rot in some cell somewhere."

Billie sucked her bottom lip into her mouth and started chewing. I knew how she felt. I wasn't so sure a brazen rescue attempt, a couple of dozen brazen rescue attempts, was the right move. Sure, I was sick over what was happening. Sick over the fact that the women in custody were likely being interrogated, mistreated. But how could we hope to infiltrate some secret facility?

"I'm not sure." Even as I said the words, I knew Neeta would jump all over me.

I was right. Neeta jumped to her knees, leaning forward like she might spring. "What do you mean, *I'm not sure?* What else is there for us to do, Miranda?"

"Don't snap at her, I feel the same way." Billie held the blankets up like she wished she could melt into the bed.

Neeta, mouth wide, stared from me to Billie, and back again. "I can't believe you two. What if it were me in there, or Ash, or my mom, or Bea? How would you feel then? You'd just let us rot?"

I tried not to sigh too loudly. I closed my eyes as I thought of how to articulate what I was thinking. "We're four, maybe five including Sara, women who have zero training in anything useful." I opened my eyes as I sat up on the couch. "Think about this, Neeta. We'll have to sneak our way into a secret facility. Who knows where it is or how difficult it would be. If this place is like I'm imagining, it's probably some sort of government black site. Do you have any inkling of the impossibility of it all? Think of how hard it is to escape from a prison. The kind of place the women are being held is probably a thousand times more secure."

"You think they're all together or separated?" A hard line formed between Neeta's brows.

"I think, logistically, that having them together in one location would make the most sense, but how would we even find out?" I shot Billie a glance, begging for backup.

Billie took the hint. "Miranda's right, Neeta. None of us are James Bond, and not a single one of us is Ethan Hunt. No way we could take on the kind of technology and firepower separating us from the other women."

Neeta scrunched up her face. "You two are forgetting one very important factor. If we train with Bea, if she teaches us all she can, and if we can find more women like us, we'll be able to take on anything or anyone. The sky will be the limit."

I shrugged. "You're not wrong, I guess. No one in this room knows exactly what we're capable of." I turned my head, gazing off at the far wall, the door to the hallway double locked with a chair jammed under the doorknob.

"Okay," Billie said in the background. "Then why do we have to make such a final decision right now? Why can't we train, learn all we can, then assess our skills? It's hard to make such a crazy decision when we don't know what we're capable of yet. Miranda is right about that. We have no idea what we can do. Bea doesn't seem unreasonable. How can she expect us to make a life-altering decision like breaking into a secure government facility without first testing our limits? Because it's quite possible that one or more of us may not make it back from such a thing."

Neeta nodded as she stared down at the comforter. "Good point. So, my suggestion is this, we take Bea up on her offer of training—I mean what other choice do we have there—and tell her that if in the end, we feel strong enough, capable enough, then, and only then, do we storm the castle."

I huffed a laugh. The reference reminded me of a line from the *Princess Bride*. It was a movie I watched a thousand times as a kid. "Deal."

"Deal," Billie agreed. "Can I turn the heat up now?"

****

Billie was the first to fall asleep. I could hear her soft, rhythmic breathing in the dark. I knew Neeta was awake, as there was yet to be any snoring.

Tossing and turning on the hard couch, I'd been unable to get comfortable. The thoughts churning in my mind were of no help. How could I relax when all I could think about was staring down the barrel of one gun or another? Not to mention that every time there was a creak out in the hallway, I froze, my heart in my throat.

Rather than torture myself any further, I pulled back the blanket and set my feet on the floor. The room was considerably warmer as Neeta had acquiesced to allowing Billie to turn up the heat.

I peeked out the curtains. All was dark and quiet.

I reached over to the paper and pen sitting on the side table. The paper was white, a nicer quality than the pad from the Taos motel. *The Stanley Hotel* was stamped across the top. This seemed the perfect time to draft another note.

Well, I can officially say the drive from New Orleans to Estes Park sucked. It sucked so big and so hard. The fact that the drive was long and boring was the least of our problems. The star of the catastrophe was Billie and her fast, nervous driving. We got pulled over. Oh, and then Billie blasted the cop and knocked him out. So, naturally, we had to drive to my house—because duh.

Miracle of miracles, my mom gave us a new getaway car, for all of twenty-four hours before she reported it stolen. I wish this was fiction. But we made it. We're here at the Stanley just waiting until morning. I still love you.

Writing the note only occupied me for so long. Whenever I couldn't sleep, a little pacing would usually do the trick. Pacing was tricky in the small room, but I didn't need a lot of space. To the door I counted eleven steps. I turned back toward the couch, following the same course. On my third pass by the foot of the bed, Neeta raised her head from her pillow.

"What are you doing? You're not sick, are you?"

"Can't sleep. Walking sometimes helps." I did my best to keep my voice low. At least one of us should get some rest.

"Gotcha. I'd join you if there was room in here." Bedsprings squawked as Neeta adjusted her position in the dark. "Want to talk about anything?"

"What could there possibly be to talk about? Nothing ever happens to us. We're just a couple of ultra-boring girls."

Neeta chuckled. "Yeah, super boring."

"Do you ever wonder why this happened to us? I mean, if Aunt Bea is right and there are only about fifty of us in the United States, then we must have some really shitty luck. What are the odds, you know?"

"Oh, I know. That very thought has crossed my mind more times than I can count. The odds must be astronomical. Even more insane is that you holed up at the same hotel where Bill and I were living. How the three of us ended up together is so beyond fateful it's freaky. I can't believe there was a time when I thought your powers were some kind of communicable disease. Like it was your fault we came down with this virus."

"Super freaky." I stopped in my tracks at the foot

of the bed. I could only see Neeta as a shape, not a fully formed being, in the dark. "And super lucky. I could have ended up anywhere. I thank the gods that I pulled into the Fleur that night. It feels like years ago, the night I checked in, terrified of a gruff Trapper, more terrified of a scantily clad Billie, shocked by the ring in your nipple. That girl, I don't even know her anymore. Hard to believe that night was only a few weeks ago."

"It does feel like years ago. I can't believe how much our lives have changed in such a short time. We could have ended up in such worse shape, any one of us. Escaping as we did seems like a miracle now, although I know it wasn't. We're a team, a unit. When one of us falls apart, the others are there to put us back together. Pulling into the Fleur was lucky for you, and lucky for us. Billie and I would have fallen apart without you."

"And I without the two of you."

****

"What is this place?" Billie asked the question everyone was thinking.

The three-story brick building was not what I had expected. Something about the way Aunt Bea had described the place on the drive there made me think *school* meant your run-of-the-mill concrete box with long linoleum hallways, but what we pulled up to was not the kind of school I had ever seen. This school looked like more of a mansion, an old one, with dark, blood red bricks covered in vines, leaded glass pane windows streaked with dirt, and a giant, darkly stained, oak door that looked like it could withstand a battering from a dragon. In short, I thought I'd not only gone back in time, but stepped onto the pages of a book.

"This is an old school, like centuries old, that's been lost to time and the elements. Lucky for us, Sara's grandfather left her this chunk of land, and this building.

It's the perfect hideaway, deep in the woods and surrounded by barbed wire fencing higher than our heads."

The place did feel secure. More secure than anywhere I had been in some time. To access the long road leading to the school, we'd had to stop the car while Aunt Bea got out to unlock a massive iron chain threaded through two tall gates four times larger than the car we drove in.

"Looks like something out of *Harry Potter*." Billie lugged my suitcase out of the boot of Aunt Bea's Gremlin, then set it on the ground to pull out her own bag.

"Wait until you see inside." Aunt Bea stared up at her home in the woods. "Plus, we're so far from the road, and there isn't anyone around for miles. There's also a perfect clearing beyond the overrun garden for practicing spells. Don't want to set the forest on fire. Fires are devastating around here."

I picked up my suitcase, taking my grandma's quilt from Neeta's outstretched hand.

"Oh, Mira." Aunt Bea took the quilt from my hands, a sad smile on her face as she caressed the patches. "I'm so glad you have this. Mom would be so happy."

Aunt Bea hugged the quilt to her body. "Well, my friends, come inside and I'll show you where you're all sleeping."

"We prefer to be as close together as possible." Billie closed the boot of the Gremlin, then moved behind me.

I wanted to echo those sentiments, but I also craved some space. As much as I loved Billie and Neeta, and I loved them more than I could articulate, I also needed a little room to breathe. Being in such close proximity for so many hours on end had me feeling a tad claustrophobic.

Aunt Bea, her long, flowy skirt dragging over gravel, ambled up the stone steps, her keys jingling in her hand. "That won't be much of a problem. This place is huge, and there are a lot of rooms to choose from. Plenty of room for all of us, plus Sara and Lou."

"Lou?" I stopped abruptly. My aunt had a man around? I wasn't sure how I felt about this. Joey and Trapper had been allies we could trust, but I'd also thought I could trust Henry, which had proven to be a mistake I'd never forget.

Aunt Bea shot me a knowing smile. "Louise. Hates being called that, so she goes by Lou. Billie and I get it down to our toes, don't we, dear?"

"More than anyone will ever know," Billie responded.

"You'll love Lou." Aunt Bea stuck the old-fashioned key in the lock. "She's seventeen, a runaway like you, Mira, and a hell of a lot of fun."

The word *runaway*, thrown so loosely around by my aunt, bit me to the quick. The sentence was a throwaway, something stupidly said in the moment that everyone is guilty of on occasion, but coming from Aunt Bea, I'd been burned.

Aunt Bea didn't seem to notice or think twice about what she'd said. Instead, she pushed the front door aside using her shoulder, stepped into the dark interior, and stood back, her arm with the quilt tossed over it thrown out to introduce the space. "Here we are. Welcome to your new home."

A rush of cool, musty air hit me straight in the face. I flinched slightly, but the sensation, and the smell, was not unpleasant. There was a hint of library in the scent—old library with dusty books covered in water-stained leather binding.

I stepped into what was the foyer. A cobwebby chandelier loomed over our heads. Floors in darkly stained wood that matched the door, lay under our feet. The walls were paneled in more dark wood covered with portraits of men and women in old-fashioned clothes. A staircase, one that went up to a half-landing then split in two different directions, was the true focal point of the room. The banisters were heavy and intricately carved. The building was all symmetry. Two rooms sat on each side of the foyer with two hallways extending just beyond these rooms, one underneath each staircase.

"Let's chat in here." Aunt Bea led us inside the room to the left. To me, it looked like what people a hundred years ago would call a parlor. There were four antique chairs, two on either side of a cherry coffee table. The large fireplace, surrounded by more blood-red bricks, smelled sooty but looked inviting. The slate hearth in front was large enough to sit on to enjoy the warmth on a cold winter's night. Dark wood beams crossed the ceiling overhead. Other than the chandelier in the foyer, which was covered in cobwebs, almost everything in this room looked clean, and freshly dusted.

"All right, dears. The place is quite large and would take hours for me to introduce to you. Explore on your own and have fun. Most of the rooms have been dusted and vacuumed. This was a boarding school, so you'll find two wings of bedrooms, along with several working bathrooms, on the second floor. Take whatever you like. Down here we have the living areas, a library, several classrooms, a kitchen, and a dining room. Yes, there is running water, and yes, it is drinkable."

"Thanks, Bea. Where do you and the others sleep?" Neeta was already edging toward the stairs.

"We all sleep upstairs in the left wing. You'll be

able to tell which rooms are vacant." Aunt Bea laid the quilt on the back of a chair.

I picked up my quilt. "Great. I guess we'll go get settled. Thanks, Aunt Bea." I breezed by Neeta, needing to take a break from my aunt.

At the top of the half-landing, I glanced down to see my aunt still standing in the parlor's doorway, watching us go upstairs. I wasn't sure what was bothering me. I just needed a moment away.

I peeked into the first room we passed. Inside was a mess of clothes on the floor. That must be Lou's room. I wasn't sure why I made this assumption, but I did. Maybe because she was seventeen and so much fun. The next door was the bathroom, the door after that was an unoccupied room. The wing was a long one with a seemingly endless hallway of door after door.

I stopped somewhere in the middle and turned a knob. There were two single beds in the room. The beds, stripped bare, sat in front of black cast iron headboards. A moth-eaten, burgundy-colored rug covered most of the dark wood floor. Walls were papered in a thick, deep green brocade. There were two wooden desks against the wall opposite the beds, along with old wooden swivel chairs and dark green covered lamps.

"Will one of us have to sleep alone?" Billie leaned her shoulder against the doorway as she looked around the room with a scowl.

"No way." Neeta shook her head. "We'll drag in another mattress, and I'll sleep on the floor under the window. There's plenty of space in here."

Neeta was right about that. The room was quite large.

"Okay, then dibs on the murder bed." Billie dropped her things to sprawl on the bare mattress.

"Seriously? No one ever wants the murder bed."

Neeta sat next to Billie's feet, kicking off her sneakers.

"I like to be able to get out faster," she said through a yawn.

I sat on my bed, happy to be as far away from the door as possible. All of the furniture may have been old, but I was happy to notice the bedding folded and sitting on the bench of the bay window—white comforters, and white sheets—all seemed brand new.

"Okay, what's up?" Billie peered over at me. "You seemed a little weird downstairs. I can't tell if you're in a daze or if something is bothering you."

"Just annoyed, I guess. My aunt called me runaway. She said *Lou is a runaway like you*. The way she said it, all nonchalant, like I haven't been through hell with my family, really knocked me sideways. Then she took grandma's quilt and put it over the back of that chair like it was hers. This quilt," I said as I pulled the patchwork blanket onto my lap, "is the only thing I have from my grandmother, the only thing I have from home. The home that is forever lost to me." I bit my upper lip, hard, to keep from welling up. Then I swallowed down the huge knot forming in the back of my throat.

"What she said was insensitive, for sure." Neeta laid back on Billie's bed. "But I'm sure she didn't mean to. She probably doesn't even realize what she said."

"Yeah, I know," I whispered, pulling the quilt up so I could inhale the lingering lavender scent from Mom's laundry soap.

Billie leaned against the headboard. "You know what? I miss Ruby. I miss all the queens. I miss how much fun we had at her club. I miss hearing you sing, Miranda. You haven't sung once since we left. You haven't hummed or anything. You used to always be humming one song or another."

"I haven't been in a musical mood."

Billie smiled over at me. "Maybe if you sang, you'd feel better. Maybe we all would."

"Another time. Promise."

"I wonder if there's a drag club in town, or at the very least a bar where we could listen to some music and dance. Let loose, a little." No one was surprised that Billie was musing about doing something that could get us in trouble.

"Bill, seriously. We can't do anything stupid. Remember?" Neeta crossed her ankles, staring over at Billie like she was about to have to reprimand a child. "It would be fun though. A lot of fun. I could go for a cocktail and a jukebox."

Billie, laying back, lifted her chin to look at Neeta. "What would it hurt, really?"

"Everything," I answered. "It's no use fantasizing about doing something fun like that. We'll just get in trouble, thrown away for an eternity."

"Not if we're in disguise." Billie was whispering as if we were nothing more than kids in cahoots.

I was the kid; they were supposed to be the adults. I made a face at Billie as I tried to decipher what she was saying. "Disguise? Like fake mustaches and costumes?"

Billie grunted. "No, silly. Wigs, glasses, things like that. Things that will hide who we are and help us to blend in with the locals."

"And where are we going to get these things, Bill? You think Bea is going to let us wander down to the store to buy some wigs so we can go to a bar, with her sixteen-year-old niece who's wanted by the law for being a witch? Girl, I adore you, but sometimes your ability to rationalize is pretty whack."

Billie ignored this comment from Neeta, continuing her fantastical thinking out loud. "Hair dye. Changing our hair would probably be a good idea anyway, right? I've always wanted to be a redhead. Miranda would make a great blonde, and you could…"

Neeta cut her off. "No one is touching my hair."

"Okay, fine. I'll find you a pair of fake prescription glasses, then. Anything to change ourselves up a bit."

"This isn't a horrible idea. I'm not too excited about being a blonde, but Billie's right, we should take a cue from other outlaws and change up our appearances. Aunt Bea would probably agree."

"I suppose," Neeta agreed. "But no bars, Bill. No nights out. We have to be smart."

"As you keep saying. You can just come out and say it. You blame me for what happened with the cop." Billie flopped onto her side.

Neeta rapped the footboard with her knuckle. "No one blames you for anything. What happened could have happened to any of us. Besides, if you hadn't blasted that guy, who knows where we'd be now, or if we'd be."

"Neeta's right, Billie. No one is upset with you. That's like saying you guys blame me for blasting Henry. We can't fault ourselves for a moment of heated self-defense. I'm sure there will be a lot more to come."

The thought of more fighting to come made my blood run cold. I was suddenly tired, again. After my conversation with Neeta the night before, I'd been able to sleep for almost six hours, not to mention the sleep I'd gotten in the car the day before. I shouldn't be so exhausted. I should be ready to go, ready to train, to move on to the next phase. Only I wasn't. I swallowed down the new sense of dread rising in the back of my throat. There would be more fighting, possibly even killing. One of my friends could die, my aunt could die, I could, too.

With thoughts of blue energy surging from my

body, being used to hurt, to kill, I collapsed on my little bed, turning my face to the wall. I buried my face in the quilt so my friends couldn't hear me weep.

Chapter Six

Somewhere in between sleep and wakefulness, an image of Aunt Bea's grimoire sprang to mind. In my dreamlike state, I watched myself, sitting in a cracked, worn leather chair flipping through the pages of the leather-bound book. Picking out one or two skills to master seemed impossible. There were too many options, too many skills I wished to possess, needed to possess. The rough-textured paper of the book made my fingertips tingle. The further I flipped through the book, the more things I wanted to learn.

"Hey, wake up. The other two girls are here, and Bea has dinner ready downstairs." Neeta poked my shoulder with her index finger. "Girls? Maybe I should say women, but Lou is underage like you." Neeta said this last part to herself as she moved away from the bed.

"Dinner? How long did I sleep?" I rolled onto my back, peering around the darkened room. The dark green curtains were pulled tight, deep shadows in every corner. "Where's Billie?"

"Downstairs."

I noticed the pile of bedding at the foot of my bed. I'd slept on the bare mattress, my quilt wrapped up in my arms like a teddy bear. Billie's bed was made, the white bedding tucked in neat. On the floor between the foot of my bed and one of the desks lay another mattress, all made up with the same white bedding.

"I must have slept through a lot." I threw my legs over the side of the bed, wooziness rolling through like I'd been drinking. Only I hadn't. "Why am I so tired, and why do I feel so weird?"

Neeta, in a fresh pair of shorts and a black polo, walked over to me, placed the back of her hand over my forehead, and shook her head. "I wish I knew. You're not warm, so no fever. Maybe everything we've been through is hitting you a little hard. Gross food and weird sleeping schedules can rough a person up."

"You and Billie seem fine." I tried keeping the annoyance out of my voice as I teetered to my feet. As far as I knew, they'd slept less than me.

"Seeming fine and being fine are two different things. Did Billie seem fine when she blasted that cop? Stop talking nonsense and let's get some food in you." Neeta marched to the open door, standing in the doorframe with an arm out like she was my formal escort to dinner.

"Fine." I let go of my emotional-support blanket to follow Neeta downstairs.

The hall was dark, lit only here and there by small, tarnished brass sconces. There were more sconces, lining the entire hallway, but only about a third held lightbulbs.

I hadn't noticed before, but the wallpaper was the same emerald green of our bedroom, textured and thick. I ran a hand along it as I walked, marveling at how soft it was to the touch after so many years and so many hands. The floor creaked under my feet. "How old do you think this place is?"

Neeta shrugged up ahead. "A hundred and fifty years, or so. Who knows? I'll tell you, it gives me the creeps. I feel like I'm being watched everywhere I go. Just being alone in the bathroom freaks me out."

"That's probably the ghosts."

Neeta shot me a look that could melt glass. "Not funny."

"Did you explore much while I slept?"

"No." Neeta shook her head, her hands shoved into her pockets. "We made our beds, put our toiletries in the bathroom, which is right next to our room by the way, and whispered in the dark while you slept. We figured we'd take a look around when we could do it together."

I was relieved. The thought of poking through the old rooms was exciting, and something I didn't want to miss out on. Although it was probably too late in the day to explore the grounds, the interior was massive and offered a night full of intriguing possibilities.

We wound our way down and around the double-wide staircase, me following Neeta as she led the way to the hallway opposite the parlor room. I would have to trust Neeta knew where she was going as the farther we went, the more lost I was.

"I thought you said you hadn't explored."

"I haven't, except that I've been to the kitchen and know where the dining room is. We did have to eat while you slept. Peanut butter and jelly. Definitely preferable to greasy burgers and fries."

The reference to our least favorite, but readily available, road trip meal left a sour taste in my mouth. I grimaced.

Halfway down the long hallway, this one covered in a peeling, slate gray wallpaper with embellished black designs, Neeta turned to the right. There sat the largest dining table I had ever seen. The heavy legs were carved to look like tree trunks, the massive tabletop, scratched and stained from over a century of use. This was a piece of furniture that would die with the house because no one would ever be able to move it. The room was paneled in dark wood, candles lit on the sideboard and bunched in the middle of the dining table, giving off a séance vibe.

Aunt Bea sat at the head of the monstrous table. The hotel clerk I recognized as Sara sat to her right, and a girl so small she reminded me of a bird sat to her left. This girl, Lou, I assumed, had hair that looked like pink air, all light and fluffy. Her expression was flat. She neither smiled nor scowled as she watched us walk in.

Billie, sitting to the right of Sara, turned her beaming smile on me and Neeta. "An actual home cooked meal," she squealed, slathering a piece of crusty bread with soft butter. "No fast food, no room service."

Around the grouping of candles sat platters laden with food. One held slices of roast chicken, another was filled with mashed potatoes, another still, overflowing with steamed broccoli and cauliflower.

"I thought the three of you could use the nourishment." Aunt Bea smiled warmly, and I forgot why I was ever annoyed with her in the first place. I sat next to the girl I assumed was Lou, while Neeta sat next to Billie.

"Neeta, Miranda, this is Lou." Aunt Bea gestured toward the girl with the cotton candy hair. "And this is Sara, who you met at the hotel desk, Neeta."

Sara smiled, nodding her head as she did so. She was older than I had thought, probably in her forties. She had a pretty face with eyes so blue I wondered if they were contacts and the longest lashes I'd ever seen outside of the falsies the queens wore at Ruby's.

"It's nice to meet you both," I said.

I again looked at Lou, who had yet to smile or even move. Lou had a serious look about her that made me wonder why my aunt had spoken of her so fondly. The only noticeable thing about her, other than her hair and the silver stud in her nose, was a tattoo on her neck. I couldn't get a good look without staring, but it looked like the tail of a dragon.

Sara, scooping some mashed potatoes on her plate, looked at me. "I hear you're a singer. I play a little piano myself."

"Cool. I play guitar."

"Wonderful. Maybe we can put on a show one

night. Alleviate some of the boredom."

"Maybe. I haven't really been in a musical mood." I wondered what Sara could possibly mean by boredom. Didn't they have a lot to do, what with training and planning a mass breakout?

Lou turned her head, not fully, but enough for me to see she was about to speak to me. "You didn't have to be so rude about it. No one cares if you don't want to sing."

I stared across the table at Neeta and Billie, whose mouths had dropped open. I slid a sideways glance toward Lou. As I opened my mouth to retort, Aunt Bea jumped in.

"Okay, everyone. Let's just eat, shall we? Sara and I went to a lot of trouble to cook for you all."

Recovering from the snide comment Lou threw at me took me a full three minutes. I sat rigid in my chair, focusing on my breathing, staring across the table at my friends. Billie was looking at her plate like we'd gotten in trouble. Neeta was looking at Lou like she'd enjoy smacking her while spearing a piece of chicken with her fork.

Hunger finally won out. I shook off the encounter, then piled my plate with every offering of food there was on the table.

We all ate in silence, the candles flickering over the paneling like the flame would devour the wood if it could.

****

"What in the hell was that?" Billie flopped into a leather chair, one that sparked recognition in me.

"Yeah, Bea made it seem like Lou was super fun, or am I imagining that?" Neeta reached under a green shaded table lamp, fidgeting for the light switch. This was the same style of lamp on the desks in our bedroom.

"You're not imagining anything." I ran my hand along the spines of books.

We'd found the library, which was every bit as impressive as I'd imagined it would be. The books were dusty, many of the spines were cracked, bindings slipping away, but there were just as many in near perfect condition as if in a hundred and fifty years they'd never been touched.

Shelves lined the walls all the way to the ceiling. The furniture, and the floors, were all the same dark wood as the rest of the house. There was a hopelessly out of date and dusty globe the size of a beach ball sitting on a stand in one corner, a brass insert fireplace in the center of the wall opposite the imposing double doors, and a mantle that held the bust of a man I could not identity with a clock that had stopped at midnight, or noon.

Two long tables sat in the center of the room, chairs tucked in all around. Two dark brown, cracked leather chairs, one of which was currently occupied by Billie, flanked the fireplace.

I could imagine students clustered around the tables, heads bent over their books while a professor, possibly smoking a cigar—there certainly was a lingering scent of tobacco mixing with the smell of musty old books—sat in one of the chairs.

"My aunt seems … off to me." I paused before the word *off* because I wasn't sure how else to describe the feeling I had that something wasn't right.

"What do you mean?" Billie brought her knees up under her chin.

I thought about how to answer. What *did* I mean? My aunt hadn't seemed like the Aunt Bea I remembered, but in what way was hard to articulate. Granted, I hadn't seen her in a couple of years. My aunt had been all over the world, meeting people from all different walks of life, studying magic. Would anyone be the same after so much adventure?

"I'm not sure. Maybe it's nothing." I took the vacant leather chair, leaning back into the soft tufting.

"If it was nothing, you wouldn't have said anything." Billie shot Neeta a nervous look, before returning her gaze to me. "Try to explain why she seems off to you."

"Well…" I gazed at the unlit fireplace. "Her reaction to seeing me at the hotel was not as warm as I'd imagined. Aside from my grandma, Aunt Bea was always the warmest person in my family. And if she was so worried about our safety, why did she leave us there last night? Wouldn't you think she'd want us here, behind a locked gate, as soon as possible? And then there's the way she called me a runaway. I get that people misspeak all the time, but the Aunt Bea I remember would never have been so insensitive. She was also weird about my quilt."

"I'll grant you that leaving us at the hotel was a little odd. I guess I hadn't really thought about it. Maybe she just wanted us to get some rest before she introduced us to the school." Neeta chewed the inside of her lip as she leaned her backside against one of the long tables. "I mean, you're right. You haven't seen her for a long time, and we're clearly in danger. And how was she able to locate you in New Orleans? I mean, really? She hasn't explained that. If she used witchcraft, or whatever we're calling it, don't you think she'd explain how she did it, even briefly?"

Billie shot out of the leather chair, jogging to the door to close us in. She slunk back, exhaustion or annoyance etching a line between her brows. "Will we ever be comfortable again, ever be safe, ever not have to look over our damn shoulders? What do we do about this? Leave?"

Neeta crossed her arms. "And go where? We're very nearly out of cash, and we have no vehicle. Oh, and then there's also the part about being wanted fugitives." She massaged her forehead. "Man, we are so fucked."

"Neeta's right." I sighed. "Not about being fucked, but about all the rest. We have nowhere else to go, not right now. The best thing we can do is stay here and learn all we can. We have no proof anything is wrong with my aunt. The years and what she's been through may have changed her like it's already changed us. So, we keep our eyes open, our backs to the wall, and we learn all the magic shit that we can. And most importantly of all, we stay close to each other. We're stronger together."

"Definitely." Neeta pushed herself off the table, then walked to the mantle where she studied the clock.

I crossed my legs, sinking farther back into the chair. "I am going to get my hands on that grimoire, though."

Neeta spun around. "What?"

I inclined my head to the side, tossing up one shoulder. "I don't buy this bullshit that we only need to master one or two things, and she'll pick what she thinks each of us will excel at. Why shouldn't we choose for ourselves? I'm tired of not being in control of my own fate."

"She's going to know you took her book, Miranda. Then she'll know we're suspicious of her."

"What Billie said."

"I'm not going to take it. We're going to copy the pages, so we have our own grimoire. Then, we can study the spells she isn't teaching us on our own."

"How do you propose we do that?" Neeta braced a hand against the mantle as if she needed to hold on for what was to come.

I smiled coyly at both my friends. "I'm going to sneak into her room and snatch the book, tonight. Then, we'll copy the pages together, furiously, and return the book. Easy."

Billie huffed an annoyed sigh. "That plan sounds anything but easy. Are you crazy? Have we all gone completely insane? She's a witch, only she knows a lot more than us. Do you really think you'll be able to sneak into her room, steal her book, and then copy all the pages, returning the book before she wakes? No way."

"Billie, come on. It's not such a big deal. If we get caught, she's not going to execute us."

Neeta frowned. "You just said she seems off to you. Maybe she won't kill us, but she might do something unpleasant."

I shook her head. "She won't. I'll play the dumb, innocent teenager. All I have to do is start crying and say that I was curious, that I just wanted to take a little peek. She'll be mad, but she'll get over it. And anyway, we won't get caught. I'm good at sneaking things. Don't forget I grew up with parents who didn't allow me to do anything. Sneaking is all I did for years."

Neeta left the mantle to start poking around. "Do you think there's paper and pens in here?"

****

We found all the paper we needed, four notebooks worth, plus an entire pack of old, but sharpened, unused pencils. it was almost as if they were waiting for us. We snuck these treasures up to our room, tucked under shirts, the pencils shoved in the back pocket of Neeta's jeans.

Aunt Bea came by our room a little before eleven o'clock. She braced herself in our doorway, her head pushing inside. "Everything is locked up for the night. Do you three need anything before I head to bed? Cocoa, or a snack?"

All three of us were lounging on our beds, pajamas on. I smiled brightly at my aunt. "No thank you, Aunt Bea. We're about to go to sleep ourselves."

"Wonderful. Tomorrow, we begin the exciting stuff." Aunt Bea tugged the door closed.

"One hour," I whispered.

Chapter Seven

An hour later, I was creeping down the hallway. We'd agreed I would go alone while Neeta and Billie waited just outside our bedroom door. That way, I could get in and out of my aunt's room easier, and my friends would be within earshot if something went wrong.

The hall was dark. There was one lone window all the way at the end, but it was so far away that any light from the night sky was no help at all to me. I couldn't risk a candle or a flashlight, so I made my way by trailing my fingertips along the thick, embossed wallpaper. There were no obstructions along the way, so all I had to do was count the doors as I passed them. My aunt's room was the third door from the stairway landing on the right, my left. The moth-eaten carpet muffled my footfalls, although the floor underneath the carpet was old and did give off a slight creak from time to time. Because of this I walked slow, slower than I'd like given the fact we had a lot of work ahead of us if we were going to successfully copy every page of the grimoire in the next few hours.

Other than the slight creaking of the floor and my breath, all was silent. I could still smell the roast chicken from earlier, my stomach threatening to growl as I hadn't eaten much at dinner with all the weirdness.

Six, five, four, three.

I was there. My heartbeat raged in my chest. Was I really doing this? Sneaking into my aunt's room while she slept to steal from her?

An ear to the door told me all was quiet within. I placed my hand on the knob, swallowing down the discomfort creeping up my spine. I knew I had nothing to fear, not really. My aunt, no matter how changed, wouldn't hurt me. My fear came from the breaking and entering, from the thieving. What I was doing was wrong no matter how you looked at it.

The doorknob twisted silently in my hand. I breathed a little sigh of relief. I hadn't thought until that moment that the doorknob, ancient as it was, may be a little troublesome, or even locked. It wasn't.

Just as I was about to nudge the door open, another door opened not far from where I stood. I sucked in a breath. There was nowhere for me to hide, and I wasn't prepared to burst into my aunt's room.

I jolted to the side, turning the knob of the neighboring door, and dashing inside. I was in a bathroom, dark and unoccupied, but only momentarily. The door opened to reveal Lou, who flicked a switch, the room flooding with light. There I stood, an awkward, sheepish smile on my face. "Hey," I said, feeling instantly stupid.

"Hi." Lou looked around the small room, all sterile white tiles. "Were you peeing in the dark?"

"About to." I laughed. "Bright lights hurt my eyes sometimes."

"Okay." Lou looked me up and down, her soft, pink hair pulled into a messy bun. "I'll use the toilet across the hall. Night." She turned the light back off before retreating.

I collapsed against the sink cabinet, my breath a little ragged. What I hoped more than anything was that Neeta and Billie stayed put. Surely, they heard something of the encounter, but if they came down the hall and ran into Lou, they'd bungle the whole enterprise.

I stayed where I was, listening hard for Lou. After a couple of minutes, I heard the door across the hall open and close, soft footfalls trail back down to her room.

Back in the hallway, I stood still, counting to sixty, five times. When I heard no other sounds, I went back to Aunt Bea's door to repeat my earlier actions.

This time, when I turned the doorknob, I was able to edge it open without any interruptions. My head went in first. Once I was reassured that my aunt was soundly asleep, I edged the rest of the way in. Aunt Bea's window was wide open, fresh air, and more importantly, light from the half moon and stars, filtering into the room. She lay on her side, her face turned away from me, giving me a measure of comfort.

Now for the hard part. Where was the grimoire? I stood in front of the half-open door, my gaze darting around the space. The grimoire was not sitting out, as I hoped it would be. Something easy would have been nice.

Since I was going to have to search for the book, I pushed the door almost closed behind me, keeping it slightly ajar to ease my escape. The nightstand contained nothing but a glass of half-full water and a romance novel. The top of the dresser was equally benign. There was nothing there but crystal jewelry and a pair of socks. I swallowed as I realized I was going to have to start digging into drawers, something I really hadn't wanted to do.

My hand trailed down the front of the dresser to the top drawer, but before I could tug at the handle, a thought popped into my mind. A memory, really. In the memory, me and Aunt Bea were sitting at my parent's kitchen table playing Uno. My aunt was telling me about her childhood, and how she'd have to hide the books her dad didn't want her reading under her bed. I smiled to myself at the thought.

Turning from the dresser, I dropped down to all fours, creeping back over to the bed. I moved the bed skirt up and out of the way, then fished around the pitch darkness. A spider was just as likely to be found as a book, this thought almost causing me to shrink away. Right before I did, my fingers grazed leather.

I nudged the book toward me, grasping it firmly in my hand.

As I made to stand up, Aunt Bea grunted in the bed above. My heart stopped beating.

This is how I die.

In a crouch, one hand holding onto the book for dear life, the other bracing myself on the metal frame of the bed, I teetered on the balls of my feet. Trying to breathe as shallowly as possible, I waited, listening for any other sound to issue forth. When none came, Aunt Bea's breathing returning to a normal rhythm, I, afraid to fully stand, turned toward the door half bent over. Then I crouch-walked, thighs burning from the exertion, to the door.

I didn't take a real, full breath until I was back in the dark hallway, the door closed behind me. I realized with a near-groan that I would have to do this all again when it came time to return the book. But that was a problem for future me. The me of now had to rush back to my own room where the three of us would take turns furiously copying the grimoire word for word.

Trailing my hand along the wall, I made it to my room in what seemed like seconds, much faster than when I left.

Neeta and Billie were at the door.

"What took you so long?" Neeta whisper yelled as they followed me inside the room.

"Lou, that's what happened." I tossed the book on the desk closest to the door.

"Did she see you?" Billie closed the door, flicking the lock for an extra measure of security.

I pulled out the chair, taking a seat while I grabbed up a pencil. "Yes, she saw me, and talked to me.

I dashed into a bathroom and pretended like I was peeing. She was also on her way to the bathroom but went across the hall instead."

"We have a closer bathroom down here. Do you think she was suspicious?" Neeta pulled out the chair from the neighboring desk.

I shrugged, opening the book to the first page. "It was hard to tell in the dark. But if she was, I don't think she would have gone back to her room without checking that I'd done the same." I placed the pencil at the ready. "Let's do this. We need every minute we have. As we discussed, I'll copy the page on the left, Neeta, you copy the page on the right. Then, Billie can take over for you in a bit, and you can take over for me after a while, and then we'll keep rotating. Ready?"

We started writing. We'd agreed not to absorb too much of what we were seeing. If we did that, we'd just get stuck and want to talk about the different spells. There wasn't time for that. We had to act like machines, copy down what we saw without thinking too much about it. There would be time later to really go over what we had in our possession.

For me, time passed in a blur while we worked. I thought of movies I had seen where the passage of time is marked by an analog clock, the hands of the clock speeding around the face, passing number after number in rapid succession.

We rotated in and out of chairs like a demented game of duck, duck goose. The hour was nearing five am by the time we finished, my fingers sore and cramped, my eyes heavy with exhaustion.

"We did it." Billie dotted her last I.

Neeta closed the book with a thump that sounded thunderous. She held it out to me. "Are you sure you don't want me to take it back?"

I shook my head. "No. I'll do the same thing I did before. Easy." The endeavor was anything but easy but knowing this and admitting this were two different things. I tucked the book under my arm and made my way back into the dark hallway.

Déjà vu.

Since there was no reason to reinvent the wheel, I retraced my steps exactly as I'd taken them all those hours ago. I made it to my aunt's door in record time.

I'm getting good at this.

Once again, I listened for any sound within. When I was satisfied all was as it should be, I turned the knob and carefully opened the door. What I saw as I stepped into the room filled me with dread.

There sat my aunt mid-yawn, a finger wiping the sleep from her eyes. She jumped as I entered the room. "Mira, what on earth are you doing?" The last word died in her mouth as her gaze dropped to the grimoire held in my hand.

Aunt Bea shot to her feet, her sleepshirt, pink with a corny saying about coffee on the front, tangled at her knees. "Did you steal that from my room?" She snatched the book from my hand.

"I…" Before I could think of what to say I was cut off.

"You were always rebellious, Mira, and I know I encouraged that in you, but stealing is out of bounds. You caught me on the one night I didn't hide it with a spell. I certainly won't be so lazy, again."

I recovered my voice. I knew if I was to regain any sort of trust with my aunt, I'd have to make this good. "I'm sorry. I didn't steal it. I borrowed it. It's just that I'm so antsy to get started, I thought I could at least read up a bit on a few spells. But I was so tired, that when I got back to my room, I fell asleep before I could read much of anything. So, really, I went to all this trouble, including getting myself caught, for nothing. I'm so sorry, Aunt Bea. I just want to learn and make you proud." I forced my voice to crack on the last word, squinting up my face like I was about to cry.

"Oh, Mira. Of course, I'm proud of you. But you went about things the wrong way. Never take another witches' grimoire. A grimoire is personal, unique to each witch. In time, you'll write your own. And as I said before, there is far too much information in this book for any one witch. You'll only need to learn a portion. Trust that I know what is best. For all of you."

"You're right, Auntie. Trusting is something I have to learn how to do again."

I knew I was tugging at the heartstrings by using the endearment of *Auntie,* and it worked.

Aunt Bea pulled me into a tight hug. "Now, go get some more rest. It's far too early to be up." With that, she gave me a gentle shove out the door.

I barely recognized myself anymore. I'd become someone who'd lost all trust in anyone outside my immediate circle, and I'd become a liar. But was lying really a bad thing when you weren't sure if you were safe? And that was the thing. Although I wanted to trust Aunt Bea with my life, Aunt Bea was my mom's sister, and my mom had betrayed me in a way I wasn't sure I'd ever get over.

I contemplated all this as I shuffled my way back down the hall for the second time.

"How did it go?"

I barely heard Billie as I edged past her. All I wanted to do was collapse on the bed, not think, not feel, just shut off my brain for a few hours and sleep.

"Miranda?" Neeta stepped in front of me, cutting off my forward movement. "You look like you've been zombified. What happened?"

A sigh, loud and ragged, escaped me. "Aunt Bea was awake. She caught me coming into her room with the grimoire, but I think we're okay. I said I wanted to learn some things to impress her but fell asleep before I could read much."

"Are you joking?" Billie whispered with vehemence. "Well, if we couldn't trust her before, now she's really going to be a problem."

"Okay." Neeta held up her hands like she was trying to reason with an angry mob. "All we can do is keep going with the plan. We go along with whatever is happening here, we trust no one outside this room, and we learn all we can from the book. But one thing we have to make sure of is that we're always aware of where we are, who's around us, what they're saying, and what their body language is telling us. It's called situational awareness. My dad was in the military."

"I know all about situational awareness, believe me." Billie crawled into her bed. "If you're with a john and you can't read a situation, well, that's just asking for problems. Are you okay, Miranda?"

I was now under the covers, only a tiny sliver of forehead showing. I mumbled that I was fine, just tired.

"I hear you. I've never been so tired. Tired of all this shit." I heard Neeta sink onto her floor mattress. "I stuffed the pages inside a slit in my mattress, by the way."

Within seconds, all was silent, and I closed my eyes, sinking deeper into the bed.

Chapter Eight

Late afternoon, the three of us found ourselves in the library.

I had managed to avoid seeing Aunt Bea all morning. When Aunt Bea was coming out of her bathroom, fresh from her morning shower, I was diving into a vacant bedroom. When Aunt Bea was in the kitchen, pouring herself some cereal, I was ducking into the parlor. Seeing her was inevitable, but I would put the meeting off as long as humanly possible.

"When are these *lessons* your aunt was going to teach us supposed to actually start?" Billie sat in the same leather chair she had before, Neeta in the other one.

I sat next to the cold hearth, ten pages from the copied grimoire in my hands. Sara was at the hotel. Aunt Bea and Lou were both in the kitchen making lunch. I felt relatively safe having the pages out, and besides that, the door to the library was locked. Had anyone come around, I'd have plenty of time to shove them inside my shirt. "I'm beginning to wonder if she's going to teach us anything. Another reason why last night had to happen."

"Super strange. Read to us." Billie tapped a finger on the arm of the chair. She'd been tapping the same spot for twenty minutes.

I went back to page one. "Okay. The first few pages are like a travel journal. This must be from her first trip, dated almost exactly two years ago, September 6th." I cleared my throat. "*I've arrived in Romania after four layovers, and a lost suitcase. My plan is to knock on the door of Raveena, the famous local witch who is believed to be very powerful, and who is renowned the world over. Witch culture is out in the open here, with witches marrying into other witch families to keep the bloodline as pure as possible. The witches are also female and are celebrated throughout the village. People come to them for help of every variety. There was no way to introduce myself to Raveena beforehand. Had I done so, there would be a trail of some kind—digital or paper. The only way to go about this will be to approach her at her home. I have no way of knowing how this will go, how she will receive me, or if she will receive me. I may have made a long, tiresome journey for nothing. Only time will tell."*

"The next entry is the following day, September 7th." I glanced nervously at the door before continuing. *"In only a few hours, I learned more from Raveena than I've yet to learn from any book. The woman is a fount of knowledge. She welcomed me into her home with open arms, and although her English was not good, and my Romanian was even worse, we managed to communicate decently well. The first thing we did was drink tea while we talked about our individual abilities—they differ slightly. She too can manipulate energy, although she doesn't show this to anyone outside her home. 'They would be afraid of me', she says. Instead, when dealing with clients, she focuses on incantations and spellwork. She says those are things they are more able to wrap their heads around. Show too much power to any one person, and they could become your enemy. Another gem from Raveena."*

"On September 8th, there's a short entry followed by a list of ingredients. The entry reads, *A man followed me to Raveena's this morning. I did my best to lose him, but as I was on foot, this was difficult. I warned Raveena when I arrived at her home, and she seemed worried. I didn't wish to bring her scrutiny, although I believe whoever follows me is from the US. He would have no immediate interest in Raveena, but the bubbling fear could spread, so I thanked her for the time she'd already spent with me and took my leave. Before I left, she pressed a torn, half-sheet of paper in my hand. Below is the transcribed spell, exactly as she wrote it, translated from Romanian.*

"Protection spell to be cast on a necklace of black tourmaline. Charge the crystal overnight by the light of the full moon. The next morning, cast your circle, light a white candle, ring a brass bell, and say the following three times—goddess, cover me with your light, hide me from evil, protect me from harm, so mote it be. Wear the necklace and recharge every full moon."

Neeta nodded, a solemn look in her eye. "I like this. Seems like a simple way to keep us out of harm's way."

"Yeah," Billie said. "We just have to find black tourmaline, whatever the hell that is, and wait for a full moon, whenever the hell that is." There was a weariness in Billie's voice that I felt in my bones. The grimoire was another hurdle, another set of tasks that may or may not help us in the long run.

"Someone's coming." Neeta jumped to her feet.

I folded the pages of the grimoire and shoved them inside the front pocket of my jeans. I'd never been more grateful for creaky old floors. "Open the door before whoever it is realizes it's locked."

Neeta was already halfway to the door. She flicked the lock gently, so it would release as quietly as possible, then tiptoed back to her chair. She sat back down right as the door opened, trying to look relaxed as if she'd been seated the whole time.

The door opened, framing Lou as she leaned a shoulder against the dark, carved doorframe. She peered around the room without entering, her gaze not touching Billie or Neeta but piercing me where I sat in front of the hearth. "This is where you three are hiding. Well, you found the perfect place. No one ever comes in here." She glanced down at her nails as if she were already bored with the conversation.

"We love this room," Billie said defensively. Saying this was a little ridiculous. Billie sounded like a child putting her foot down, but I understood the sentiment. We felt safe in the library, cocooned away from the rest of the world. This room was a refuge, a place where we could talk about anything without fear of being overheard. Little did Lou know what we were reading and discussing before she interrupted.

"Great." Lou looked up from her fingernails but didn't look at Billie. Instead, she again glanced at me. "Anyway, Bea is ready for all of us on the back porch. Bea calls it a verandah." Lou huffed what may have been a laugh but sounded more like a grunt as she stepped back, disappearing around the corner. I heard her footfalls, the floor protesting, as she walked away.

"Okay, let's get out there." I grabbed hold of the arm of Neeta's chair, hauling myself to my feet.

"I'm dying to know what she's going to say to us or if she'll teach us anything." Billie was already halfway to the door.

"I'm hoping she'll surprise us, that we'll get right into what we need to know."

A girl could hope.

****

The back verandah, as Lou said Aunt Bea called it, was a brick raised porch, covered by a darkly stained wooden roof that provided shade and shelter. The roof was held up by carved spindles, half of which seemed ready to collapse inward. Ivy grew around the spindles, around the railing and up every surface of the exterior walls of the old school. I tried not to think of spiders and centipedes, but with so much available greenery to hide within, imagining creepy crawlies was not difficult.

What had held up the best after all the years was the pristine brick floor of the porch and stairs, which led down toward a winding path. The path appeared to split into three separate avenues. One ended about half a football field from the back of the school at a stone door that looked like it may have held a garden within. Another trailed off into the distance, beyond the tree line, and another led to a dried-up hole in the ground, which from where I stood, appeared to have at one time been a swimming pool.

Aunt Bea and Sara sat at a large iron table with four matching chairs, two steaming cups of tea in front of them. Two other chairs, clearly brought out from the dining room, sat at either end. Aunt Bea sat in one of the dining chairs, a brand-new whiteboard behind her. In her hand she held a dry-erase marker.

Sara sat to her right, Lou to her left.

Maybe we were about to learn something real, after all.

"Sit down, friends." Aunt Bea gestured to chairs, then to a pitcher of lemonade in the center of the table and a small platter of cookies and sandwiches. "Help yourself to food and treats." Aunt Bea's gaze lingered on me a little longer than was comfortable. Her mouth tipped up slightly, but there was an expression in her eyes I couldn't read. Disappointment, probably. There was no way to know if she'd told Lou or Sara, the woman who seemed like her closest companion, about the previous night or not. All I could do was smile sheepishly as I took my seat, my gaze on the table, the pitcher of lemonade, anywhere but on my aunt.

Neeta took the opposite end of the table, me to her right, Billie to her left. I wanted to feel, with all my heart, like the six of us were together, one whole team, but I couldn't help but feel as if it was us versus them with myself, Billie, and Neeta as *us*.

When everyone was seated, Billie helped herself to lemonade and a cookie. Aunt Bea smiled her warm, gentle smile. "Most of the history will be repetitive for Sara and Lou, but they've insisted on attending today's lesson."

My stomach twisted. *History*. The history of what we were, and why this had happened to us was interesting, surely, but what we really needed to know were practical ways to protect and defend ourselves. If we were truly going after the women who'd been taken, the history of witches wasn't going to help us much, and the longer we waited, the more likely it would be that the women would be harder to locate, harder to get out.

A foot kicked me under the table. Since both my friends were staring at me with pointedly wide eyes, it was impossible to tell whose foot rammed my shin. What was clear was that they were both thinking the same thing I was.

Aunt Bea, seemingly oblivious to the ire at the end of the table, rose from her chair, uncapping her marker as she did so. "As far as I've been able to tell from my travels and study, there have always been witches, from the beginning of time. A witch can be born from any bloodline, and this is what has made us so difficult to trace through history. There is no one established bloodline, no familial connection between witches. Witches can be related, as Miranda and I are, but this is not always the case. There have been bloodline witches, of course, but this is changing. More often than not, witches are now born randomly. There is no particular planetary alignment, no phase of the moon, nothing that seemingly connects."

"Lucky us." Neeta crossed her arms over the

table. "So, this is totally random?"

Aunt Bea, sympathy softening her features, said, "Possibly, yes. What's different this time, as opposed to any other time in history, is there seems to be more of us. I have a theory about this, but mind you, it's only a theory." Aunt Bea hesitated as she stared off toward the pool.

"What's your theory?" Neeta prompted.

Aunt Bea cleared her throat. "I believe that it's very possible all women are capable of magic and have been since the beginning of time. I believe the vast majority of women either repress this magic subconsciously or keep the magic to themselves. Historically, women have been suppressed, have been given a set of rules by which to conduct themselves, rules that men have not had to follow. This societal suppression may have extended into the subconscious mind of women around the world, keeping the magic at bay. But today, women are wearier, more fed up than ever. This may be why the magic is coming out so unpredictably, especially at first, so uncontrollably. Perhaps more of us are now being triggered, sick and tired of the repression through the millennia, sick and tired of acting properly, of being quiet. The powers that be are certainly paying attention now."

"To our detriment," Neeta interrupted.

"To our detriment. But we're rallying, Neeta, and I have every faith that we'll take control of what's happening. Now, about the powers. Our powers are also different. The electrical power that we possess, the blue light we manipulate from our bodies, this is new, and more intense than powers of the past. There is so much more than the light, than the energy. Have you ever had a premonition? Wished for something and it came true? Do you collect rocks, shells, pinecones? Do animals come to you? These are characteristics of the witch. We are attracted to nature, and nature is attracted to us. The light is harder to control, especially at the beginning when this was happening to women who had no idea what was going on. If you've been following the news at all, you'll probably note that there are fewer reports of new witches, probably because the women who are developing now have more information as to what they are, and more ability to isolate themselves before they're found out."

"So, tell us more about the electrical aspect." I shifted in my seat. "What does that mean, exactly?"

Aunt Bea inclined her head. "I'm still learning about this myself. But essentially, we are able to generate electricity within our bodies and manipulate this energy. We can also affect the manmade electricity that surrounds us on a daily basis. Have you noticed lightbulbs flicker when you're nearby? You probably didn't realize this, but you have the power to turn a light off and on or blow out the bulb if you wish. As far as I'm aware, one or more of us could blackout an entire city."

"Wicked," Billie breathed.

"Wicked, indeed." Aunt Bea put her marker to the board. She wrote the word electrical and underlined it. "The power is not uncontrollable, not unwieldy. You call it forth as you need it, and the rest of the time, it sleeps like a kitten in the sun. As far as I'm aware, there is an infinite source of power in each and every one of us. If you were wondering why a group of powerful women is so frightening to the world, now you can understand why.

"But we'll get more into this later when we start learning how to control and manipulate our personal power. Today is about the history of witchcraft, which affects us all as much as the blue light, for we all have the power to create spells, enchant objects, make potions. These are as much a part of what we are as anything else, and in learning the history, there may be clues as to why we're in our current predicament."

"Are we going to learn about the Salem witches?" Billie dropped crumbs from her cookie as she interrupted.

Aunt Bea made a face, shaking her head. "Our history reaches back to the beginning of time, as I've said. Besides, the poor women and men of Salem, who lost their lives so cruelly were not true witches. They were as non-magical as the chair you're sitting in. Victims of a fanatical religion."

We had been on such a promising path, learning about this electrical energy and what we could do with it, that my stomach lurched at the thought of having to go backward. I understood the importance of learning history but didn't see what good this would do when we faced such present dangers. More and more as I sat and listened, I believed I'd done the right thing by stealing the grimoire. What the three of us needed were actionable steps we could take in the fight that was to come. I understood this now more than ever. A fight was coming, and it was going to be big, and it was going to be bloody. Aunt Bea was right about one thing, how could the powers that be suffer a bunch of women with untold power to walk unchecked on the streets? We'd never be allowed to live everyday lives, even though, I was sure, that was all any of us wanted to do. An everyday life was no longer a possibility for any woman who possessed this blue energy inside them.

Ash sprang to mind. Ash with her smile, and her sweetness. Ash who wanted to be a chef, who wanted to do something with her life. What life could she have with me? Me who would always be hunted, always be running, fighting for my very existence? I could offer Ash nothing but pain and uncertainty.

I tucked this feeling away as I scribbled a note on

a napkin in my lap.

We're at an old, abandoned school with my aunt. As if this life could get any weirder. It's kind of cool here, but the vibe is off. All I know is I miss you. I miss your voice. You and the stage were the things that grounded me. Maybe I'm just being dramatic. I miss you anyway.

I stuck the napkin in my pocket.

Sitting in that hard iron chair, listening to my aunt drone on about the history of witchcraft, my heart shattered into a million pieces. We'd never be together, and the sooner I wrapped my mind around that, the sooner I'd be able to forget Ash and everything we could have been.

****

Two hours later and I thought my brain may be melting. My aunt was taking us on a very long, very boring journey through history. The worst part? We had only made it to the birth of Christ.

Tears of joy almost sprang to my eye when Aunt Bea announced, "Why don't we take a break. This stuff is a little tedious, and I can see more than one set of eyes glazing over."

We didn't need to be told twice. Any reprieve I could be given from an actual conversation with my aunt was to be leapt at. I jumped from the hard chair, my rear end sore, my back in knots, and grabbed Neeta's hand. I inclined my head to Billie and took off for the *Secret Garden-esque* stone gate.

We walked in a single file down the path of cracked stone, overgrown with weeds and grass.

I heard Billie whisper, "Where are we going?", but I didn't turn around to answer. Billie would figure it out.

As it was late afternoon, the sun was starting to make its way farther west, bathing us in shadows from the dense forest around us.

The garden—I assumed the area contained within the high stone walls was a garden—would likely be brown, as overgrown as the path from years of neglect. But we would be alone, away from prying eyes, and more importantly, listening ears.

The gate, a creamy, crumbling, beige stone, was as covered in ivy as the walls. I stepped up to it, running my hands over the tangle of vines as I searched for a way to open the door, eyes open for biting beasties.

"Here." Neeta pushed back a swath of ivy. The handle, an iron doorknob, was oddly on the opposite side of where I was expecting to find it.

Neeta gave the door a shove, but it wouldn't budge.

A glance behind told me we were being watched by Aunt Bea, Sara, and Lou as the three of them remained sitting on the back verandah. "What are they doing?" I said this under my breath, a smile on my face.

Billie turned her head, then quickly looked at me. "They're giving me the creeps. Open that door."

"Not moving." Neeta grunted as she again tried pushing open the door.

I pressed my shoulder against the ivy-covered stone. "All of us on three. One, two, three."

Together, we shoved into the stone gate with all our might. The teamwork was successful. The gate gave way by a fraction of a degree. As we gave the door one final shove, the stone opened far enough for us to squeeze through one by one.

Neeta was the first to step through, followed by Billie, then me. I did everything in my power to not look behind at those we'd left. I was sure the audience was still there, watching us as we disappeared inside the garden.

"Wow." I emerged into what seemed like a different world. I'd never been to England, but this garden, or more accurately, what the garden probably was once upon a time, was what I imagined every English garden to look like.

"I know, right? It's just like *The Secret Garden*. My mom read that book to me when I was little." Neeta picked her way around an overgrown bush.

"If this is *The Secret Garden*, then that means we can bring all this back to life, right?" Billie bent back a small branch, which snapped off in her hand.

"Maybe we can do it magically." I took in my surroundings. There were larger trees, still green with life, though in bad need of a trim, that provided the perfect amount of shade. The gravel paths were weedy but still visible. There were shrubs that had turned brown, rose bushes that had shriveled, but there were also statues, a little green in places from slimy moss, but beautiful, nonetheless. There were stone benches sitting along pathways and under trees. We walked down the center path past statues of what appeared to be Greek Gods, men with heavily muscled bodies wrapped in togas, women, lithe and lovely, draped in the long flowy dresses of the time. The path took us right to the center of the garden where we found an old, mossy, dried-up fountain, another statue at its center, this one a centaur.

"Whoever created this place loved ancient Greece." I stared up at the centaur, his tail in mid-swish, one foreleg about to step forward, his human face turned toward the sky.

"It's very cool." Billie sat on the deep edge of the fountain. "I'm not sure which place I like better, this garden or the library."

"This is another place where we can slip away for some privacy. It's good to have options. Should we take out the pages and keep reading?" Neeta opted for a seat on a bench a few feet from the fountain under the shade of a golden-leafed maple tree.

"Sure." I stuck my hand in my pocket but didn't pull out the pages. I just held it there for a moment. I thought about how I missed the fun of being in New Orleans. Even through the stress, the uncertainty, we still had so much fun, at Ruby's, at The Trumpet, walking down Bourbon Street. We needed some fun now, something, anything to lighten the heaviness wearing us down. "I think Billie was right."

"I was? About what?"

I passed her a sly glance. "About finding a bar, about going out to have some fun. I want to blow off some steam, to get away from the watchful eye of my aunt. I want to dance, and I really, really need to sing."

Billie's eyes lit up like a full moon. "Yes."

"No." Neeta huffed, not moving off her bench. "Can you two focus for five minutes? We cannot go out. We're not safe out there, even if we try to disguise ourselves. And besides…" Neeta crossed her legs. "How would we get there? We'd have to steal Bea's car. You don't think she'd find out in one hot second?"

Gravel crunched off to the left, startling me out of my skin.

Lou stood in the middle of path, her arms crossed over her chest. "I can help with the car."

"Were you spying on us?" Neeta jumped to her feet, craning her neck to look behind Lou.

"There's no one here but me." Lou tightened her arms, her cotton candy hair moving in the breeze. "And no, I'm not spying. I didn't realize this was a secret meeting only for the three of you. I saw you come in and have been wanting to check this place out, too. Sorry, I'll leave you alone with your little mean girls' club." Lou made to turn around.

"Wait," Billie called.

I reached out a hand to grab Billie's arm. The gesture was meant to silence her, to convey that we didn't want Lou hanging out with us, hurt feelings or not. We didn't know Lou. How could we trust her? We couldn't trust anyone.

Billie shrugged out of my grasp, ignoring the unspoken comment. "We're not a mean girls' club. We're just used to being a unit, that's all. Come sit with us. And tell us more about what you meant, about helping with the car."

Lou eyed Billie suspiciously. After a moment, seemingly satisfied, she dropped her arms from her chest and wandered a little closer as if she hadn't a care in the world. "Well, there's another car, a car that doesn't belong to Bea, in the garage at the very end of the drive."

"There's a garage?" Neeta's voice sounded uncertain.

Lou nodded. "Yeah, if you keep following the main drive in front of the school, you'll find it. It's huge. Sara says it was a carriage house at one time. Anyway, there's a car in there. The keys are in the visor."

"How old is it? The car won't help us if it's eighty years old and doesn't run." Neeta narrowed her eyes. She trusted Lou about as much as I did.

"The car isn't eighty years old, maybe twenty or so, but not eighty. And I know the engine runs. Sara used it not long ago. The car belonged to her grandpa or something."

"This won't work." Neeta was the one to now cross her arms. "We'd have to drive it back down the driveway, past the school. With all the gravel we'd make too much noise." She was shaking her head as she spoke as if to make sure we understood how stupid this idea was.

"We could roll it past." Lou offered up the suggestion with a shrug.

"Lou has a point, Neeta." Billie beamed a smile on Neeta meant to thaw her icy exterior. "Besides, safety in numbers. Four is better than three, *and*," Billie said, laying a loud emphasis on the word *and.* "With the APB out on us, the local authorities will be looking for three women, not four. We'll throw them off." Billie raised an eyebrow to accompany her smile.

"Bill," Neeta started.

I knew I was going to have to combine my voice with Billie's to make Neeta crack. I, too, turned my brightest smile on Neeta. "Please. Oh, Neeta, please. I have to sing. And if I don't get away from this closed-off feeling, I might burst. We all know what happens when one of us bursts, so really, this is for the benefit of everyone here."

Neeta rolled her eyes. "Boy, the two of you can lay it on thick. Just where do you think you can sing around here? Remember that we have to look inconspicuous."

"There's a karaoke bar over on eleventh." Lou stepped even closer to their circle, dropping her voice. "Sara's mentioned it before. I have a fake ID, so we can go there, even though she says no one ever gets carded."

"Perfect." Billie clapped her hands together. "We don't want anyone scrutinizing our ID's anyway."

"What about the fact that we all look pretty identifiable." Neeta was not letting this go without a fight.

"We'll where hats or something." Neither was Billie.

"I have some hair dye," Lou offered. "Pink, blue, and straight bleach. Sara has a red wig she bought in case she needs to change up her look. I could sneak it out of her closet."

I wasn't sure about the hair dye, but it was probably a good idea, regardless. "I can lighten my hair with some bleach, I guess."

Billie ran a hand through her short blonde strands. "I'll wear the wig. Is it a natural red or a red that could draw attention?"

"Natural."

Neeta grunted, drawing all eyes to her. "I'm not going to get out of this, am I?"

"Not unless you want to let us go without you." Billie winked at Neeta, knowing full well what her answer would be.

"You two aren't going anywhere without me."

Chapter Nine

Before I knew what was happening, we'd agreed to steal, or borrow, according to Billie, a car that didn't belong to us to sneak off the school's property. Our destination? A karaoke bar. Three wanted females, and one extra, were sneaking off to hang out at a bar in the wide open. *Stupid.*

I sat in the dining room chair, spearing a roasted carrot with my fork. My stomach twisted in nervous, but also excited, knots. The thought of getting out and doing something normal, well, normal for us, made my jitters hard to contain. Stupid or not, I couldn't wait until lights out. My goal of the day of avoiding a one-on-one conversation with my aunt had so far been successful. After another day or two of avoidance, I hoped the matter would be forgotten.

Aunt Bea sat at the head of the table, as usual, Sara and Lou in their spots on either side of her.

"Miranda?" Aunt Bea's voice jerked me out of my thoughts.

Mid-chew, I glanced up at my aunt. "Yeah."

"Sara was asking if you'd sing for us tonight. I have an old guitar upstairs."

I was taken a little aback. A nervous coil twisted through my stomach at the thought of having to sing for Sara and my aunt. I wasn't sure why. My aunt had heard me sing numerous times over the years. Still, something blocked me from accepting. "I'm not sure that I'm ready to sing again, not yet."

This wasn't exactly a lie. Although I had agreed to the karaoke bar, I was still unsure whether or not I'd actually get up and sing. Not only could singing draw unwanted attention, but there was also another implication as well.

The last time I'd sang was to Ash from the stage at Ruby's. I thought about singing to her for the first time at the club, how nervous I'd been. I thought about our date at City Park and how I'd sung to her as we fantasized about living in our own little world. I squeezed my eyes shut, dropping my fork on the plate with a clang.

"Miranda, what's wrong?" There was genuine worry in the voice of my aunt. "If you don't want to sing, no one here will make you."

"I'm just, I have a headache." I stuttered out the words, shoving the chair back with a little too much force as I stood. The chair tipped backward and fell against the floor. "Sorry, I need to go lie down."

I bolted from the room. As I caught the corner of the door frame with my hand, propelling myself out into the hall, I heard muffled voices behind me. The only sentence that stood out was Billie saying, "She hasn't felt well all day. I'm sure all she needs is sleep."

I was grateful for the intervention. The last thing I wanted was Aunt Bea to come to our room to check on me. If she thought I was going straight to bed, hopefully she'd stay away.

****

Three hours later, the three of us were preparing to sneak out. Lou was to meet us at the front door, and from there, we'd all go outside together. I'll admit to a little thrill of excitement. Nothing could compare to going out in New Orleans, but I needed something to make me feel normal. I think we all did.

Our clothing was limited as we'd been in a rush to leave the Fleur. I had left behind my two vintage dresses, along with most of my other vintage treasures, which still left a sick feeling in my belly. To me, those dresses were irreplaceable. Not wanting to wear the same old pair of jeans I'd been wearing for days, I dressed in my vintage plaid schoolgirl skirt, which given the surroundings was apt. The weather here was so drastically different than it had been in New Orleans, so instead of my little tank top and Mary Janes, I pulled on a black sweater and a pair of black rainboots found in the coat closet downstairs.

Billie wore her blue babydoll dress with an ivory cardigan thrown over. She strapped on her sandals, the only shoes she had besides her sneakers, and pinned back the sides of the long red wig with her plastic butterfly clips. Lou had pilfered the wig from Sara's closet sometime during the day.

Neeta wore her black Bermuda shorts with her black polo shirt and the only pair of shoes she'd brought—her black Air Force Ones, which were looking a little dusty.

There hadn't been time to color anyone's hair, certainly not without drawing notice, so I pulled my long, dark hair into a ponytail and wrapped a yellow headband scarf around my head to cover as much hair as possible.

Neeta wound her braids into a bun, then covered them up with a cool black fedora borrowed from Lou.

Our disguises would have to do.

Out of all of us, Billie looked the most different, and hopefully this would be enough to help us blend in.

Billie stared at herself in the mirror, pinching her cheeks to draw color. "I look so ridiculously pale in this wig. I didn't think it was possible to look any whiter, yet here I am."

"You look great, and you know it. You could shave your head and look beautiful." Neeta was tying her last shoe as she sat on the edge of my bed. "Maybe you should keep that wig and wear it the next time you see Joey. Give him a little thrill."

"Oh." Billie groaned. "Why did you have to

mention him? I miss him so much. The batteries in my vibrator are almost dead."

My mouth dropped open, but I recovered quickly. Nothing should surprise me anymore. "You brought a vibrator?"

"Of course. A girl can't be expected to live without her vibrator. Especially when her boyfriend is in another state. Besides, it's small, and fits very neatly in the front pocket of my tote bag. Everyone should have a vibrator."

"Okay." Neeta stood up, moving Billie away from the mirror. "Let's all stop saying the word vibrator please. It's time to go."

"Fine." Billie buttoned up her cardigan. "Lead the way, Miss Prude."

Neeta snorted a soft laugh. "I think we all know that I'm no prude. Come on."

****

The hall was as quiet and dark as the night before. We walked in a single file line with Neeta at the front. I took up the rear, my hand trailing along the thick wallpaper, the same as before. Touching the wall grounded me, made me feel as if I were tethered to the earth. Without the touchstone, I would have felt as if I were being swallowed up by the dark void of the hall, as if I were trying to escape an endless tunnel.

When we reached the end of the hall, passing the room I knew to be Aunt Bea's, I held my breath. We agreed to each pass the room one at a time, to put less stress on the old floor and minimize creaks.

Neeta went first. I had to crane my neck around Billie's tall body and could only see Neeta as a shapeless form in the dark. Before she'd gone too far, Neeta became invisible, seemingly swallowed by the void.

Billie reached back with a hand to grasp mine. We

squeezed hands. Then Billie dropped my grasp and raised on her tiptoes. She moved away from me, then became another shapeless form in the dark.

Since it was impossible to see, I closed my eyes and counted to thirty. I'd heard nothing from the other two, so our idea to ease the pressure on the floor had seemed a sound one. I stepped forward, on my tiptoes as Billie had. It wasn't until that moment I realized I'd been holding my breath. My lungs needed air, but if I exhaled then sucked in a breath, I ran the risk of being too loud and alerting my aunt to the situation.

There are people who can hold their breath for minutes.

I decided not to exhale, no matter how much my lungs burned. I refused. However, the burning in my lungs propelled me forward a little faster than I'd meant to go. As I stepped from one foot to the other, without giving the floor time to adjust to my weight, the boards underneath me gave off a loud creak. I had no choice but to pause. I'd made a mistake, and I knew it. As I froze, two steps away from Aunt Bea's door, I strained to listen for any movement within, every muscle in my body tensing, my heartbeat thudding in my ears. After a few seconds, I relaxed. Nothing stirred anywhere on the second floor.

I resumed walking, more careful this time, so as not to stress the floor again. By the time I reached Billie and Neeta, I was lightheaded from holding my breath. I let it out through my mouth in a slow exhale, inhaling as quietly and gently as I could even though I wanted more than anything to take a huge gulp of air.

Billie grabbed my hand, and we turned to descend the staircase. When everyone was safely down, Neeta stopped, Billie running into her back. Neeta whirled around. "Are you okay?"

I could just make out the features of her face in the starlight from the high transom window over the door. "Fine. I can't help it if the centuries-old floor squeaked underneath me."

Neeta screwed up her mouth, then sighed. "I know. It's just that I didn't like this from the beginning. We cannot get caught. This is the last time I sneak out of this creepy school with you two. From now on, we're following the rules to the letter."

"Well, we're here now." Billie's profile stared off into the dark parlor. "Where is Lou? Shouldn't she be here by now?"

My stomach pinched.

You're just nervous.

I tried shaking off my nerves. Lou was probably late. Maybe she'd been detained by something and was unable to get out of her room on time.

"She'll be here," I reasoned, my gaze on the dark staircase, waiting for the small figure of Lou to descend.

"Oh, she's right here." A lamp clicked on in the parlor, flooding the room and the floor at our feet in light.

Dread washed over me, nausea rolling through my belly. My knees went weak, and I had to reach out to Billie to steady myself.

Standing in the center of the parlor stood my aunt in a green t-shirt and pajama pants, her arms crossed tight across her chest. On the sofa to her left, sat Lou, her face in her hands, her back heaving with silent sobs.

She looked up at us, her pink hair stuck to the side of her wet face. "She caught me coming out of my room. I tripped and made too much noise." She heaved a ragged breath. "I'm so sorry."

Neeta mumbled something that sounded like, "*Great.*"

"Please come sit down, ladies. Join the middle of

the night fun." Aunt Bea backed up so that she stood in front of the parlor's fireplace, her arms still tight around her body. Her face was a mix of emotions—her eyes flashed anger, but her mouth was turned down into the saddest frown I had ever seen. "I'm not sure if I can convey my disappointment. I know the three of you feel apart from the group, but I'd hoped that would dissipate the more time went on, the more you became comfortable with us and your surroundings. The fact is, there cannot be cliques. There cannot be fractioned groups. We are a team, a family."

I felt the scrutiny of my aunt's gaze. I squirmed as if I were in the hotseat. "We weren't being cliquish. We were taking Lou with us. Even though that was obviously a mistake." I felt mean saying the words, but once they were out of my mouth, they were out.

My aunt tapped a foot against the carpet. "You were taking Lou because she knew about the car in the carriage house. Don't pretend you were including her for any other reason, and please don't interrupt me again." Aunt Bea heaved a heavy sigh. She raked her hands through wiry hair, which had begun to look wilder of late. She stared at the coffee table laden with heavy books.

She'd never spoken so sharply to me before. Even when I'd been caught returning the grimoire.

Aunt Bea leveled me with a sharp glance. "This is the second time you've upset me in less than twenty-four hours, Mira. I really don't know you at all anymore, do I?"

I didn't know how to answer the question or if my aunt even wanted me to, so I kept quiet, dropping my gaze to my lap. What was the point of arguing, anyway? Doing so would not help the situation.

Aunt Bea sighed, continuing. "You three are not prisoners here. I realize it may feel that way, but you're not. We're in hiding, all of us. You don't think I go a little stir crazy from time to time? Of course I do. But now, more than ever, we have to remain vigilant, aware of outside eyes and what they're seeing. Had you made it to the bar tonight, don't get me started on the fact that Miranda is sixteen and Lou is seventeen, you'd have put all of us and what we're doing in danger."

"What are we doing, exactly?" Neeta asked.

I looked up to see Neeta melted into the back of the sofa, her arms as tightly crossed as Aunt Bea's.

"I don't understand the question." Aunt Bea narrowed her eyes slightly.

"I mean, what are we doing here, exactly? Learning about the history of witches is not very helpful or practical for what we're up against. You said you wanted us to bust those other women out of jail, or wherever, and we're learning about some witch from two hundred years ago? We need to be learning practical magic, spells, and shit, and how to control and direct our powers." Neeta had finally voiced what should have already been said.

Aunt Bea raised her chin, her eyes narrowing further. "I've had some time to reconsider our plans. After reflection, I've concluded the best course of action is to start from the beginning. You can't learn magic without a good foundation. You can't learn anything without a good foundation, any teacher will tell you that. We'll get to spells and shit later."

Billie cocked her head, a furrow forming between her brows. "What about the women, though? We can't leave them much longer. Who knows what will happen to them."

Aunt Bea huffed a laugh. "You seem awfully concerned for someone who didn't want to rescue them in the first place."

Billie jumped to her feet, her hands on her hips. "I was scared. I wasn't sure we could do it, but I came here, didn't I? I came here with the intention of helping them escape."

"And you think we can do it? What gives you the confidence now?"

"I guess thinking that you had all this wonderful stuff to teach us. That's what gave me the confidence, but now, now this place just feels weird. You feel weird." Billie dropped her hands.

Neeta scooted along the sofa until she was closer to Billie, her gaze never leaving Aunt Bea.

I was on alert, too. Billie had voiced what we'd been saying in private. Something had changed with my aunt. What had changed was anyone's guess.

Lou continued sobbing quietly into her hands while all this was going on. I hadn't taken the girl for such a sensitive soul. Lou had been rather hard and abrasive with us. Maybe I had been making too many assumptions. Assumptions about my aunt, and assumptions about Lou.

"I feel weird?" Aunt Bea's face, before, stern and sad in equal measure, now just looked sad. Her eyes softened and drooped, matching the line of her frown. "Is this how you feel, Miranda? You've known me the longest. Do you think I seem weird?" Aunt Bea stared at me with the saddest puppy dog eyes I had ever seen.

I wasn't completely sure how to answer, but I knew one thing, we'd told enough lies. If we were going to get to the bottom of whatever was going on, I'd have to be honest with my aunt. I crossed my legs, smoothing out the edges of my skirt. "Maybe, a little. We came here not only to seek safety, but to learn how to defend ourselves, how to help others. You seem to be avoiding teaching us anything of value."

"Well." Aunt Bea leaned against the hard stone mantle behind her. "I'm sorry I've been such a disappointment."

Guilt washed over me, but before I could reassure her, Aunt Bea continued. "The three of you have only been here a very short time. I understand you're all young, and I understand you've been out there in the thick of things. Of course you're ready to learn everything right now. All I can do at this point is assure you that I have a plan for your education, and if we skip through the beginning lessons, you may miss things of importance. If this is not amenable to you, you may leave at any time. As I've said, you're not prisoners. I only ask you don't do anything to lead others back to the rest of us. But it is my sincerest wish you will stay and learn, stay and eventually fight. The choice is yours." With that, Aunt Bea pushed herself away from the mantle, propelling herself right past me and the others, out into the foyer. She disappeared into the darkness of the hall. The only clue she'd ascended the stairs was the telltale creak of the floorboards.

The three of us stood and sat in shock for a good couple of minutes, Lou still sniffling into her hands.

Finally, Billie sat down alongside Neeta. "I mean, we're obviously staying, right?"

"Where else are we going to go? I've said this before. No matter what's happened, this place is still our best bet." Neeta rubbed her eyes as she spoke.

"Right." Billie nodded. "And in the meantime, we still have the…"

"Billie." Neeta stopped her before she could say anything else in front of Lou. "It's time for bed. Come on, everyone."

Billie's face went paler than usual as she glanced at Lou, realizing the mistake she'd almost made. "Yeah, bedtime."

Lou cleared her throat, wiping the dripping of her nose with the back of her hand. "What do you still have?"

Although, apparently distraught, Lou had picked up on the one thing we'd rather she hadn't heard. She peered at us each in turn through wet lashes.

I smiled, bouncing to my feet. "We still have an interest in learning. That's what Billie meant, I'm sure."

Billie laughed, pushing a curl behind an ear. "Miranda knows exactly what I was going to say, as usual."

Lou nodded. "Well, that's important when you're at a magical school." Some of her former snark had reentered her voice.

I glanced at Billie, then inclined my head toward the foyer. I heard a click behind me as someone turned off the lamp, casting all four of us, once again, in total darkness. I reached out a hand, finding the banister to feel my way back up the stairs. The sooner we were back in our own world, away from the eyes and ears of the other women in the house, the better.

Walking down the hallway in the dark was becoming second nature, and this time, I was back in my room in record time. I never once glanced behind me to see who followed. Once the light clicked off in the parlor, where else was there to go but up?

Kicking off the boots, I unbuttoned my skirt, letting it fall to the floor in a heap. I kicked it aside as I walked, only wanting to fall into bed and forget the encounter with my aunt had ever happened.

Behind me, I heard the door shut. The lamp that lived on the table between my bed and Billie's flicked to life, revealing Billie sitting on the edge pulling off her sandals.

Neeta kicked off her shoes in the same manner I

had before falling onto her mattress-bed fully clothed. "Well, that was bizarre." She pulled off the fedora, flinging it across the room.

"Sure was." I slid under my covers, pulling the sheet up to my chin. I wished I could disappear into the bed and never be found again. "Tomorrow won't be awkward at all."

Billie groaned as she yanked her dress off over her head. "I hate awkward. I never know how to act or what to say."

"Clearly, as you almost gave away the fact that we have the grimoire's spells," Neeta whispered through clenched teeth.

Billie's face fell. She laid back in the bed, pulling the covers over her underwear clad body. "I didn't mean to."

"I know," Neeta said by way of apology. "We have to be careful. Which is why hanging out with Lou will be dangerous. We'll have to keep her at bay, even if it is mean."

"You're right." I closed my eyes, the light from the lamp making my head throb. "We have to stick to our original pact. It's the three of us against the world. Yes, we can learn alongside and work with the others, but we cannot share ourselves too deeply. There are too many unknowns. And we can never, never share that we have the grimoire. Those pages are for our eyes only."

"More spy shit," Billie said one second before the light clicked off.

"More spy shit." Neeta rolled over in her bed.

Chapter Ten

I didn't feel like I'd slept at all, but I did dream. Although the dream was less a dream and more a series of strange images, like some sort of David Lynch inspired nightmare. I saw myself dressed all in black, a limp woman whose clothes were in tatters slumped against me. I saw smoke or possibly dust from debris, and most frightening to me of all, I saw a building, an entire wall of which had crumbled to the ground, leaving a gaping wound, rubble piled all around.

I woke in a cold sweat, more tired than I'd been when I fell asleep.

We'd found a scrap of paper under our door that morning. On it was our schedule for the day. I figured this was Aunt Bea's way of speaking to us as little as possible after her feelings had been so clearly hurt the night before. At least she wasn't freezing us out completely.

Since Sara was working an early morning shift, we weren't beginning until noon.

"I say we learn the next spell." Neeta knelt by her bed, piling up laundry that needed to be washed. "Days keep passing, and in the meantime, we haven't learned anything from Bea. Other than that, we're not prisoners, but actually we are."

I stepped into the same jeans I'd worn for days, then buttoned a flannel shirt. Summer was sliding into Fall, the temperature cooling, the leaves changing. "You're right. We have to press on. Let's head to the garden and work there."

"Don't forget Lou found us in the garden yesterday. Maybe we should find someplace more private. Say we're going for a hike or something." Billie towel dried her wet hair, her eyes red rimmed with exhaustion.

Neeta shook her head. "Who knows how long it will take us to find a suitable place, and we have to be close by and ready for Bea's so-called lesson. The garden is a good idea. We'll close that heavy stone door behind us and rig it with something to alert us to nosy neighbors. All we need is a string and some tin cans."

After sneaking through the house, we found everything we'd need in the kitchen. I felt guilty when we emptied three cans of beans into the trash, but these were desperate times. I could worry about the wasted food later. Billie found a small hammer and a box of nails in a junk drawer.

While the three of us had been creeping from our room down to the kitchen, we'd passed by the parlor where we heard Aunt Bea and Lou talking in low voices. I figured Lou was getting more of a lecture after our escapades the night before. I felt sorry for her. Maybe we should have invited her to learn from the grimoire with us, but I quickly came back to my senses. Neeta was right. We could only rely on each other.

Together, we bolted from the back door to the garden, me looking over my shoulder every few feet. There was no one watching us that I could see. Maybe we'd get lucky this time and actually have a private moment.

Me and Neeta muscled the stone door open. This time, after slipping inside, we shoved the door all the way closed. There was a moment of anxiety as I realized we were trapped inside the high walls. If we were unable to open the door from the inside, we'd find ourselves in some trouble. I wondered how long and how loud we would have to scream to alert the others we were trapped.

Neeta dropped her backpack, pulling forth the

three empty cans and a long piece of twine. She wound the twine around the half-opened lids, tying each one in place. When she had her rudimentary alarm system jimmy rigged to her liking, she handed one end of the twine to Billie while she held the other.

While they held the cans loosely across the closed door, I took a nail and the hammer, hammering the knotted ends of the twine into the cracked mortar between the stones of the garden walls.

We stepped back to admire our work.

"It isn't beautiful, but the system should work." Neeta closed her backpack, leaving it alongside the door. "If anyone tries pushing their way through, those cans will cause a racket."

I pulled the next lesson from the grimoire from my back pocket. "Let's do this. We don't have a lot of time."

The spot next to the fountain was just as it was when we first discovered it. The golden leaves of the well-established trees were the perfect frame for the handsome face of the centaur at the center of the dry fountain.

"We should name him," Billie said as she gazed up at the statue. "He looks like a Rex to me."

"Then Rex he is." Neeta smiled, shaking her head.

The day was a cool one with clouds overhead obscuring the sun, and a cool breeze that, despite the drop in temperature, felt good. Fresh air in general was welcome to me as I'd suffered through the summer humidity of New Orleans. A pang of longing hit me square in the chest. Although I'd hated the heat, the wetness of the air, I'd loved New Orleans with everything I was. The city had felt like home to me within such a short amount of time. Not only had I fallen in love with the old buildings, the ancient trees, and above all, the music, I'd fallen for the people who had welcomed me with open arms. I'd felt more myself in New Orleans than I'd ever felt anywhere else and in so short a span of time. Before my thoughts could turn to Ash, I swallowed all this down, something I was becoming pretty good at, and took a seat on the edge of the fountain.

Billie had brought a flannel blanket from the closet in our room, and this she spread on the dirt strewn pavers surrounding the fountain. She and Neeta sat down, cross-legged, in front of me as if I were the teacher about to teach her students a new lesson.

Had I known them any less I may have felt awkward. As it was, they were now closer to me than family. Any sense of awkwardness had long since vanished.

I smoothed the paper on my knee and began reading. There was no time to waste.

"After backpacking my way through India, I have learned much about focus of power. What follows is what I have gleaned from months of study, months of conversations with many fellow witches. *Focusing power, I've learned, is the most important fundamental to a witch, after protection. There are many ways to focus power, and often these ways will differ from witch to witch, but the easiest, quickest way to focus and direct power is through natural material. Stones, crystals, even a scrap of bark or a fallen leaf. As long as the material has come from the earth, it can be used. Over time, the witch will no longer need any object to focus; all she needs is within her. But for the beginner witch, having a touchstone, whatever it may be, will help them immeasurably. I have learned that the power within us can be held indefinitely. It need not explode forth from us as is so often the case when the power first emerges. Our light can be calm and placid always. We only need to understand it, to learn to focus it, then the calm will descend. The object, collected by the witch, can be held in one hand, whichever is non-dominant, or can be worn around the neck, leaving both hands free. Once focused, the power can flow in a number of ways, the most notable of which is directly through the palms of the hands. However, something most witches do not discover for some time is that the power can also be directed through any one of the four elements—earth, air, fire, water. All the witch need do to direct the power through the earth for example, is to kneel down, pressing one hand into the ground. Similarly, to direct power through water, the witch need only touch the source of water they wish to use to their will. To direct power through the air, the witch must hold one hand high above the head, focusing not only on their power, but on the current of the air as well. To direct power through fire is more difficult. The witch can't plunge a bare hand into a flame, but they must place their hand as close to the flame as possible. This is the most dangerous use of the elements as some degree of burning will occur. But before the witch can do any of this, they must first find a natural object and practice how to focus the power. Below are step-by-step instructions on how to accomplish this very important task.*

One—find an object that speaks to you. This object can be any natural material. Keep in mind that although a witch can change out objects at random, it is useful to choose an object that will last the test of time. Therefore, stones and crystals tend to be the best materials. Leaves and twigs, these things can be used, but they will not last. These items are best used in a pinch. A witch can almost develop a relationship with her object, so choose well for the sake of longevity. To do this, simply take a walk outside, focus your thoughts on your powers and what would work best for you. Choose something you are drawn to, preferably an object that is pocket-sized.

Two—take the time to sit with your object. This is best done in solitude. Work the object in your hands. Hold it, stroke it, meditate with it.

Three—while sitting, still in a meditative state, hold the object in one hand. With the other, practice calling forth and holding your light. Do not direct the power yet, simply hold it, be one with it, feel it as a part of you. As important a part of you as your heart or your lungs.

Four—when you feel ready, hold out your hand and practice sending out the light by a small degree, then pull it back. This will seem impossible for a new witch, but it can be done and is one of the basics of control. You are in control, always. While sitting, breathing deeply, your state calm, open your palm with your arm held out, allow the light to travel a small distance from your body, then, focusing clearly on the light, continuing to breathe deeply, call it back, pull it back. This will take some practice and is possibly the most difficult part of this lesson to master. Do not be discouraged. Keep trying.

Five—once you have mastered this level of control, you are ready to further unleash your light. There is no distance that you should not be able to recall your light from. You are capable of recalling your light until the moment it hits the intended target. Practice allowing your light to wander farther and farther from you before recalling it. This will get easier the more you practice, until one day doing so will seem the easiest thing in the world.

Six—once you feel as if you are in complete control of the power within you, allow your light to hit a target. I'm sure it goes without saying that witches do not harm animals or people unless threatened. Our light can kill, can destroy without mercy. This is not something to be taken lightly. Take care where you aim. A good starting place for target practice can be a large boulder or even a bale of hay. Use what you have. You can control how intense your light is, meaning over time, you can learn how to stun with a blast or how to destroy. Don't forget to always be breathing, always to be inside of and aware of your body.

Seven—emotions are good. One thing new witches will discover is how hard it is to control the light when they are emotional. Feeling and accepting our emotions can actually help us free our minds and hearts. Do not be afraid to feel even when those feelings are sad or dark. It's when a witch keeps those emotions too tightly in check that disaster can occur. You will never learn to control the light, control the power, without first identifying and accepting how you feel. Laugh, cry, scream, don't keep anything inside. Only when you learn to let the emotion flow, and not be afraid of it, can you be in true possession of your light.

Keep this in mind above all—these powers are ancient. They will lift us up if we let them. Do not be afraid."

I glanced at Neeta and Billie, still sitting like cross-legged children in front of me. The cool breeze lifted the hair off the back of my neck, a shiver rocking my body.

"This is going to take us forever." Billie's eyes looked close to watering. She blinked quickly, her gaze leaving my face, dropping to her lap.

A pit dropped in my stomach. I'd been thinking the same thing. We'd only been at the school a few days, but the time had seemed to stretch interminably. Sulking would get us nowhere. If we wanted to be self-sufficient, the only way was forward. "This will take some time. There are several parts to practice, but we can't give up now. We can do this. Just look around us. There are so many natural objects in this garden."

Neeta's shoulders squared as she rose to her feet. "Miranda's right. Everyone up."

I scooted off the lip of the fountain, my feet firmly underneath me. "I think we should each walk in a different area of the garden. Do as the book says—breathe deep, focus your thoughts, pay attention to the world around you, and the right object should make itself known."

Billie took Neeta's proffered hand to stand with us. She didn't look as sure but nodded her head just the same.

Without speaking, I turned to my right, edging along the fountain and deeper into the garden.

The air was warmer farther in where the cool breeze was blocked by the trees and overgrown foliage. I kept to a gravel path, overgrown with weeds, my mind focused on my breath, my body, and the garden. Despite the years, possibly decades of neglect, there was green amongst the brown, color by way of forgotten flowers, blooms peeking through dense weeds. With some work, the garden could again be beautiful, was beautiful still. The walls had kept out the larger animals who would have been delighted with the feast.

The walk was a comforting one. As I walked, I kept my mind clear, focused on the beauty around me. I trailed my hand over the wild top of what was probably once a neatly trimmed hedge. The leaves poked the soft flesh of my palm. I allowed the feeling to reach from my hand all the way to my shoulder. I continued touching the plants as I walked.

At the end of the path, I came to a small, circular

clearing, sucking in my breath at the sight. In the center of the circular path stood a statue of a woman. Her dress was drapey in that classical Greek way, her face serene, a soft smile on her lips. But it wasn't the statue that had taken my breath away. It was the dozens and dozens of sunflowers, in full bloom despite the late season, that bordered the clearing.

The giant blooms were as tall as I was. I went over to one, cupped my hands around the bright yellow petals, and inhaled. In a second, I was transported back to the Fleur de Lis, the scent of the sunflowers Ash had given me surrounding me with the smells of summer, bright and fresh. Ash grinned from ear to ear, that heart meltingly happy smile, turning me into a pile of mush. The heat coming off the pavement of the parking lot in waves was nothing to the heat I felt being so close to her. It was a heat that had cooled to near frigid levels now that we were so far away from each other.

My throat tightened, my chest crushed with an unseen weight. I was about to squeeze my eyes shut, about to swallow down the knot forming at the back of my throat, when I remembered what the grimoire said about emotion. Emotion was not the enemy; emotion was the key to control. I had to allow myself to feel this sadness, this pain. I had to embrace every aspect, let it flow through me, unafraid of what this feeling may spark within.

I stood back from the sunflower as thoughts of Ash washed over me. Instead of fighting them, instead of keeping the memories at bay, I rode every wave. I choked on a sob as the tears flowed, my palms warming. My knees bit the gravel as I dropped down, bending the face of the sunflower down with me. I pressed my face into the warm seeds, heedless to the bugs that may be crawling within, and allowed myself to cry, and then cry some more.

"Miranda?" Billie's soft voice came from somewhere farther down the path.

Still, I did not cease crying. I heard the crunch of gravel behind me, followed closely by the soft touch of a hand on my back.

Billie sank to her knees alongside me, her hand rubbing my back in small, gentle circles. I was reminded of Ash, once again, how whenever she touched me, she stroked my flesh in tiny circles. This last remembrance almost broke me in two. I released the sunflower to dive my face into Billie's chest. Billie wrapped her arms around me, her breath warm over the top of my head.

"Keep crying, honey. Cry until you're spent." Billie's voice, I noticed, sounded raw, gravelly, as if she, too, had been through the wringer.

After a few more minutes of heavy sobs, I wiped my face with the back of my hand, moving away from her to sit on my rear end. The gravel was sharp, but I didn't care. I sniffed, my face still wet.

"I've written a few letters to her. Letters that I don't think I'll ever have the chance to send her. I can't do anything that would put her at risk."

"That's lovely, baby. I should do the same, but I'm shit at expressing myself. What I need is to hear his voice. If I could just hear his voice once, I think that would help me keep going."

"I'm guessing you were in your own feelings, about Joey."

"You got it. I bent down to smell this pretty red flower. Something I'd never seen before. Anyway, it had this faint almost cologne-like scent. I immediately thought of the first night Joey and I spent together. The night we didn't have sex, we just talked. Talked until dawn. I felt so safe that night, so, I don't know, important. Does that sound dumb?" Billie gazed down at her lap.

"That sounds anything but dumb." I took her hand, offering a squeeze of reassurance.

"I'd never felt that way before. Up until that moment, I only ever felt like, this is maybe a little crass, but I'd only ever felt like a hole, something to be penetrated, to be used, then left. Joey made me feel like this diamond, like I was worth something, worth his time, worth his respect." Billie returned the squeeze.

I noticed that in Billie's free hand, she held something tight.

"What is that?"

"Oh." Billie smiled at me, her eyes, a bit red, sparkled all the same. "I found my object. Right after I stopped crying." Billie opened her hand. Clutched inside was a small black stone. "It looks like it might be obsidian, or something. I don't know. I'm not exactly a geologist. All I know is that it's pretty and it fits perfectly in my palm."

"It's perfect. You could easily make it into a necklace." I grimaced as I stared at Billie's perfect stone. "I haven't found anything."

"You have to look around. Look now. I'll leave you. I just wanted to make sure you were okay. Time to start practicing, I guess." She winked an eye, kissing the back of my hand before releasing me to stand.

I watched as she strode away, my friend's gait a little more assured than it was when we started.

I went back to focusing on my breath, reminding myself why I was here, alone in this part of the garden in the first place. Still sitting in the ragged gravel, I calmly looked around me. I wasn't sure how long it would take to find my object, maybe Billie had gotten lucky, but I wasn't going to get discouraged. It wasn't until I gazed back up at the sunflower, following its long, thick stem all the way to the dirt, that I saw a stone, brown and shining in the filtered sunlight. I snatched it off the ground, turning the object over and over in my hand. The stone was smooth to the touch with long streaks of amber, yellow, and orange running down the longest side.

"Petrified wood," I whispered to myself. Many years ago, I'd been hiking with my parents when my dad found a piece of petrified wood very similar to what I now held in my hand. My dad had given the wood to Mom, which she had placed in the middle of her dresser. That piece had been much larger than the piece I now held. My piece was the perfect size not only to hold in my hand, or stash in my pocket, but it would be the perfect size for a pendant.

Now, I could begin practicing.

****

I sat with the light dancing in my palm for several minutes. I tried to be mindful, which wasn't too difficult in the quiet of the garden. I breathed, centering my body and focusing as clearly as I could on my power.

One thing I realized, as I sat with my ball of light, was that the sensation became less and less bothersome. Where before, the light almost felt like electricity coursing painfully through my body, it now felt like nothing more than a pleasant warmth nestled in the palm of my hand.

The first time I released the light it leapt to a sunflower, igniting the stem upon impact. I jumped to my feet, throwing down the burning flower to stamp it under my shoe. The air became scented with singed greenery.

Not wanting to do that again, I sat longer with the light before releasing it the second time. The second the light felt as if it was again going to go awry, I bore down, breathing with a deep grunt, my hand stretched out to call the power back. By some miracle, it worked, the light returning to my hand. Although I was sweating, shaking from the effort, I felt some sense of real accomplishment. We were getting somewhere.

Elsewhere in the garden, my friends were practicing with their own powers. All was mostly quiet, although the quiet was broken a time or two by loud exclamations, a swear word here and there, and more than one smell of smoke.

After some time, I lost track. A jingle of cans somewhere in the distance alerted me to the fact that someone had entered the garden.

I jumped to my feet, wiped sweat from my forehead with the back of my hand, and shoved the piece of petrified wood into the front pocket of my jeans. I patted the back pocket that held the lesson from the grimoire to make sure it hadn't fallen out and heard a reassuring crinkle.

"I'm guessing you three must be in here," Lou called out.

I made my way to the front of the garden, my stomach, for some reason, a little in knots as if I was nervous. Along the way I ran into Neeta, who reached out a hand.

"Oh my god," she whispered. "I found the prettiest stone, and I think I'm actually making progress." Neeta pulled a red stone from her pocket.

"That looks like the red sandstone of Garden of the Gods. Good find." I was happy we'd all found our touchstone. Moving forward would be much easier. A lightness almost came over me until I remembered Lou was waiting for us somewhere, likely with a scowl on her face.

"Yeah." Neeta didn't take notice of the furrow between my brows. "I had a good cry over missing my mom. When I sank down to my knees, there was the stone."

When we reached the front of the garden, there was Lou standing with Billie. Billie had a weird smile on her face.

Lou's arms crossed over her chest, and the narrowed set of her eyes told me all I needed to know. Lou was annoyed with us, and I couldn't care less.

"You're late for lessons." She turned her back on us, kicked aside the broken string of cans, and slipped out the half open door.

Billie shrugged and made a cringe face before following Lou out. If Billie was thinking the same thing I was, and I was pretty sure she was, we hadn't been late for anything. In fact, we were miles ahead of Aunt Bea's so-called lessons.

Chapter Eleven

The morning light streamed through the half open window, warming my hand as it lay on the white comforter. I lay awake, my eyes not yet open, but my mind racing. The day before had been one of extreme highs and lows. The highs of the day took place within the walls of the garden, control of our powers now an almost assured reality after reading and practicing the second lesson in the grimoire. As far as I was concerned, we now had two of the most important tools we would ever have in our arsenal—protection and focus. All three of us had in our possession a tangible tool to help us channel our energies. This alone was huge.

The lows had come during Aunt Bea's lecture, another long, dry, boring affair where she described in detail, for two hours, the persecution of witches during the Middle Ages. The entire lesson was pointless. Not only that, but she'd also practically glared at the three of us the entire length of the lecture, as if our presence was painful to her. This was my aunt, my family, the woman I'd rushed to for comfort, for safety. Aunt Bea was so changed, so strange, that I didn't know how to proceed where she was concerned. On the one hand, I'd already been dragged through the mud by my family, so should I really be surprised by this treatment? But on the other hand, how could I not be? Aunt Bea had never been anything like my parents. The Aunt Bea of old would have laughed off my attempt at sneaking out. Sure, things were different now, safety was a concern, but the Aunt Bea I knew wouldn't have been quite so angry. She would have been warmer, kinder.

Just when I decided I didn't want to face another day under Aunt Bea's scrutinizing glare, better to sink farther back under the covers, a hand shook my shoulder.

"Miranda, have you seen Billie?" Neeta shook me relentlessly.

I turned over, my eyes opening for the first time that day. A blurry world met my eyes, which I tried my best to blink away.

"No." I wiped crust from my eyes. "She's probably in the bathroom. You know how she likes to take a twenty-minute shower."

"She's not in the bathroom, any of them. She's not anywhere on the second floor or the first. I've been all over. I even went out back to the garden. Nothing." A note of panic had entered Neeta's voice.

I bolted upright, my chest tight with tension. "You don't think?" The question was left unfinished. The only thing I could of was that Billie snuck out to call Joey.

"Of course, where else could she be?" Neeta didn't have to say it. We were both thinking the same thing. "Yesterday was difficult for all of us. We each felt the pain of missing our loved ones. Billie must have felt it so acutely she couldn't stop herself. No shock there. That girl never thinks too far ahead." Neeta sat down hard on Billie's bed. As she did so, something crinkled under the covers.

She jumped back off the bed, stripping the comforter back. Sitting on Billie's pillow was a piece of paper. Neeta snatched it up.

"Don't be mad. I just have to hear his voice." Neeta read the note, her voice flat and tired.

"Billie, damn it." I pushed back the covers, wearily heaving myself from the warm bed. "She probably took the car from the garage, so what can we do? Walk into town on foot? We don't know the first place to even begin looking." The impossibility of the situation almost sent me back undercover.

A sharp knock on the door sent my stomach straight down to my toes.

Neeta shot me a look, fear in her widened eyes.

Before I could open my mouth to answer the knock, my aunt's voice called out. "School is in session early today."

To my horror, Aunt Bea turned the knob, opening the door. She scanned the room with a glance. "It's a mess in here. You three should really clean up a bit."

"You got it." I tried my best to sound natural, leaning a hand on the footboard of the bed.

Aunt Bea continued looking around the room, her gaze landing on Billie's empty bed. "Where is Billie?"

"Billie?" I asked, stupidly, the very opposite of natural.

"Yes." Aunt Bea narrowed her gaze. "Where is she?"

Neeta made an *umm* sound, before speaking, saving me from having to think of something to say. "She was up early, couldn't sleep. I think she went for a walk, probably in the garden."

Aunt Bea tossed long hair over a shoulder. "I'll never understand what the three of you see in that decrepit old garden. Smells like death and rot to me."

The last thing I wanted was for my aunt to start exploring the garden, so I said, "Yeah, it's pretty gross in there." We needed the secret haven all to ourselves.

"Well, get yourselves ready for the day, gather up Billie, and then head to the dining room. We're going to get started over a late breakfast." Aunt Bea turned her back on us and left the room.

Neeta sprinted to the door. She peeked her head out, then closed the door softly.

She joined me back in the center of the room.

"We're fucked. We may as well pack our shit, because once Billie is found out, Bea is going to throw us out on our asses."

Admitting Neeta was right felt like failure. I sank down on the edge of the bed. "Maybe she'll make it back in time. Billie is street smart. She knows how to sneak back into a house."

Neeta was dressed and ready for the day in a pair of shorts and a polo shirt, her usual New Orleans clothes. With everything going on, I needed to be dressed, too. When Neeta didn't answer me or make any further comment, I reluctantly moved off the bed to rifle through my suitcase. I'd been wearing the same couple of things for days and needed something fresh. From the bottom of my case, I pulled a pair of red and black plaid pants and a thin black turtleneck.

"We'll need to get you some warmer clothes if we're going to stay here much longer," I said as I walked past Neeta to head to the hallway. "I'm going to the bathroom, then we can figure this out."

The initial feeling of urgency had passed. There really wasn't much we could do. We had no clue where Billie had gone or when she would be back, which unless she got into trouble, she would be. All we could do at the moment was wait her out. If too much time passed with no Billie, then we'd be forced into action. What that action was, I had no idea.

In the bathroom, all white and green tiles, the fluorescent lighting too bright, I took the world's fastest shower. I dressed, combed my hair, then left it hanging wet around my shoulders. It was when I was putting some moisturizer on my face that I heard the commotion.

I poked my head out into the hallway but didn't see a thing. I was sure the noise had come from the vicinity of our bedroom, so I dashed next door to investigate, my wet hair dripping onto the turtleneck.

Inside our room, all was confusion. Billie sat on her knees on the floor, rocking back and forth, tears pouring through the fingers that covered her face.

Neeta was crouched next to her, trying to calm her and shush her at the same time.

Lou stood next to the door, chewing on her lip. She pulled me farther into the room, shutting the door behind us.

"What is going on?" I asked.

"Ask Lou." Neeta was rubbing Billie's back, speaking softly in her ear.

I turned to Lou, my eyes wide in the universal sign for tell me what the hell is happening.

Lou's body shook with her breath. "I was out walking and was startled out of my skin by a car coming down the drive. I see it's Billie, and she's driving so erratically that she's practically all over the road. I flagged her down, and she stopped the car, allowing me to get in the driver's seat. I pulled the car off the drive as far as I could. There was no way we were going to get it back in the carriage house this late in the morning. Bea would see us for sure. Anyway, Billie was a mess, tears and talking a mile a minute about stuff I couldn't understand. I pulled her out of the car and practically shoved her the entire way up the hill until we got to the house. We snuck through the front door, me praying every step of the way that she could remain quiet until we got up here. I'm telling you, I've never been so freaked out in my life, but we made it."

I didn't know what to say. This wasn't the first time Lou had helped us. Why she continued to look out for us, when we'd been standoffish at best, was a mystery to me. Guilt bit at my insides, shame causing my eyes to cast downward.

"Thank you for helping her. You didn't have to do that."

"We're all in this together, aren't we? I'd hate to see you guys kicked out for something stupid." Lou stuck her hands in her pockets. "I'll leave you guys alone now. I just wanted to make sure Billie was okay."

"Wait." I looked up, reaching out a hand. "You don't have to go."

When my hand grazed Lou's forearm, she smiled. "Cool."

On the floor, Neeta seemed to finally have Billie in a calmer state. Billie shuddered, her back heaving with her breath, but she had stopped openly sobbing and was now only weeping. I pulled a box of tissues off the bedside table to hand to her. Billie pulled out a wad to wipe her face.

"Okay." Neeta took her own deep breath. "Can you tell us what the hell is going on now?" Her words were harsh, her voice gentle.

Billie swallowed, her red, wet eyes, glistening with tears. She looked up at me, then over at Neeta. "I talked to Joey. It's bad." Her voice cracked, tears again sliding down her face. "Billie, what?" Neeta's hand still lingered on Billie's back.

"Right after we left, Crystal was taken into custody." Billie looked back up at me. "And the day after that, Ash was taken."

The world slipped out from under me. I would have hit the floor had Lou not jumped to my side to offer a bracing arm around my waist. "It can't be. Why would they take them? They don't have powers."

Neeta began crying alongside Billie, her arm pulling Billie tighter.

Billie's face was one of concern, pain, and anger, all mixed into one terrifying expression. "Joey wasn't able to get many answers. He wasn't there when Crystal was taken, but he was at Ruby's when they came for Ash. He thought quickly and pretended to be her uncle, hoping they would give him information. They didn't tell him much, but they did tell him where they were taking her for a temporary hold."

"She'll disappear. They both will. They'll be lost." I sank against Lou's side, my breath heaving as if I'd just run a marathon.

"Joey sounded so helpless on the phone. He apologized to me, actually apologized for not being able to do more." Billie's tears had ceased and now she had an almost dazed expression on her face, Joey's helplessness transferring to her.

"I don't want to piss anyone off, especially when emotions are high, but whoever this Joey is, he *is* helpless. There isn't anything anyone can do until we, as witches, are ready to stand up." Lou continued bracing me up, for which I was grateful, but one look at Billie's face and I knew she was about to blow.

Billie's brow knotted, her mouth a hard line. "Joey is not helpless. I didn't mean it that way. He was at Ruby's to meet with Ash and the others about Crystal. They were going to try and find her and get her out. Even if they wouldn't have succeeded, at least they were willing to act, to try and do something. What are we doing but sitting around this great big school listening to Bea drone on about witches who lived five hundred years ago? At least the three of us—" Billie stopped.

Neeta's head snapped up, giving Billie a small shake in the universal sign for shut the hell up.

"At least the three of you, what?" Lou prodded.

I got ahold of myself, moving out of Lou's hold. I stepped over to Neeta, sinking down alongside my friends. "At least the three of us want to learn more. It's just been hard with Aunt Bea not teaching us anything useful."

"Right." Lou crossed her arms, leaning against Billie's footboard. There was an expression on her face I couldn't quite read. This was the second time we'd covered one of Billie's near slips. I wanted to befriend the girl, to be able to trust her. We'd just been burned so many times. Trust did not come easily.

"I'm going back to New Orleans." Neeta turned on her knees, crawling over to her bed.

"You're going back to New Orleans?" Billie's voice was sharp, biting. "I thought it was the three of us against the world."

Neeta didn't look at her as she grabbed her backpack and began shoving her few clothes inside. "This is major, Bill. I can't speak for anyone else."

Billie shot to her feet with such ferocity I was startled backward. "I don't need you to speak for me, but if you think I'm staying here in this creepy mausoleum while you go home, you've got another thing coming."

"I'm going too." I stood, my feet a little unsteady underneath.

Billie was already packing her things, throwing blankets and pillows around in her haste.

I looked at Lou, still leaning with her arms crossed against Billie's bed. What would Lou do? I couldn't help but wonder if she'd tell on us, although that seemed unlikely at this point. All we could hope for was that Lou would remain silent. A distraction would be even better. Even though Aunt Bea had said we weren't prisoners, a prison is exactly what the school felt like.

I smiled, realized quickly my smile would appear fake, then dropped the pretense and just asked the question. "Lou, do you think you could distract my aunt in the back part of the house, or even on the back porch, so we can get out the front with our things? I don't want to put you in an awkward position or anything, so I totally get it if you say no." I added the last part hastily, not wanting to seem like I was using Lou, which I supposed I was, just a little.

"No," she said, matter-of-fact, her stance not shifting in the slightest.

Not that I could blame her, but I was stunned all the same.

Billie shot me a look over Lou's shoulder.

I shrugged at Billie. "Okay, no problem. I get you not wanting to get in trouble for us." I offered Lou a small smile before moving to my bed. I bent down to retrieve the suitcase, all the while wondering why Lou continued standing in our room without moving.

"I can't distract Bea," Lou continued behind me. "Because I'm going with you."

I almost dropped my suitcase. Neeta, on her knees, zipping up her backpack, jerked her head around. "You can't go with us, Lou. We appreciate it, really, but this isn't your problem."

That's when Lou dropped her arms. She turned, so she was fully facing us. Her face was more sad than angry, the downturn of her mouth defeated and pleading. "Of course this is my problem. This is everyone's problem. The more of us who stand up to this bullshit, the better. Maybe if we stand up, we'll set off a chain reaction and more women like us will come forward and step from the shadows. You don't think I'm sick of hiding in this place? I want to be out there fighting as much as all of you. I'm coming, and that's final."

"Fine." Billie was the first to speak. "I don't really care who comes, as long as we get moving. We have a hell of a drive ahead of us."

"Good." Lou jogged to the door. Before going out

into the hallway, she glanced over her shoulder. "I'll throw some things together, then stash my bag in the downstairs closet. I'll ask Bea to meet me in the dining room. I'll say I have to tell her a secret, that will get her attention. Then we can run out the front and grab the car."

The second she was out of the room, I looked at Neeta and then Billie. "We'll have to share with her that we have the grimoire. It would be helpful to read some more of it while we're driving. Best not to waste that time."

"Let's worry about getting out of here first." Neeta slung her backpack over her shoulder. "I'm going to grab our stuff from the bathroom. Let's be ready to go in fifteen minutes." Neeta left the room while Billie and I finished stuffing our things away.

When my suitcase was packed and snapped shut, I spread my hand over my grandmother's quilt, still laying over the bed. The blanket wasn't the most practical thing to lug around. If I was smart, I'd leave it, give my aunt what she wanted in the first place, safe in the knowledge that at least the quilt would be taken care of.

"Take it, Miranda." Billie zipped up her bag behind me. "It's easy to carry and it's nice to have in the car for sleeping."

I tossed a grateful smile over my shoulder.

Fifteen minutes later, the three of us were milling around the room, bags packed, waiting on word from Lou. When the small girl burst through the door in a rush, without knocking, all three of us jumped about a mile out of our skin.

Lou was out of breath. She held a large tote bag in one hand. "Okay, I'm heading down to stash this in the closet." She held up her bag. "Then I'll grab Bea and ask her to meet with me in the dining room, I'm pretty sure she's finishing up breakfast in the kitchen. We'll have to move fast. She won't stand in the dining room forever waiting on me."

"Believe me." Neeta's eyebrows raised to the heavens. "We can move pretty fast."

"Cool. Give me three minutes, then head down the stairs." Lou turned.

"Wait," Billie called. "We haven't eaten, and money is low. We probably only have enough to pay for gas. Maybe try to grab some food, whatever you can."

"I'll do my best." Lou rushed out of the room as swiftly as she'd rushed in.

We stood in silence, listening to the house. Part of me would miss the place, the quiet mystery, the dark corners, the creepiness as Billie called it. I would miss the library and the secret garden, I would miss the comfortable bed, and the relative safety. What I wouldn't miss was the oddness of my aunt, how I barely seemed to know the woman anymore, and I certainly wouldn't miss her horrible history lessons. We'd come all this way, and for what?

The grimoire.

We did have all the knowledge we would need from the grimoire, the pages of which were stashed in the inside pocket of my suitcase. I used to believe that everything happened for a reason, a sentiment drilled into me by my pious parents. Maybe the reason we'd come all this way, traveled so far, fear and anxiety dogging us every step of the way, was simply for the grimoire. We'd already learned so much from it. Surely there would be even more to learn over the next day and a half as we made our way back to New Orleans.

I had no doubt we would drive straight through. We had to. Stopping overnight would be too dangerous. Too many people could see us, could turn us in.

"It's time." Neeta shouldered her backpack, nodding to each of us in turn. She led the way out the door and down the hall.

Chapter Twelve

We made our way to the main landing of the staircase, following behind Neeta in a single file. We crept down the hall just as we had the night we stole the grimoire. Being now more intimately acquainted with the school, the loose floorboards and frays in carpets that could cause someone to trip were imprinted on our brains.

We waited on the landing. Neeta leaned over the railing, Billie standing behind her. I waited as if in a daze to be told when to bolt, my suitcase in one hand, the quilt hanging over my free arm. Seconds clicked by on the grandfather clock at the foot of the stairs, dust particles visible in the rays of sun streaming through the high windows.

After what seemed like not enough time, Lou bounded into the foyer, craning her neck up as she jogged across the wood floor. "Now," she whisper yelled. In one hand, she held the handles of a reusable grocery bag, filled to the brim.

Neeta sped down the stairs first, me and Billie right behind her. Neeta grabbed the grocery bag from Lou so she could retrieve her packed clothing from the hall closet. All of this took less than two minutes but felt to me like hours. Billie opened the front door and stepped out. I took one last look behind me, waiting for Neeta and Lou to exit before following.

The house seemed to groan around us, every movement we made stressing floorboards and straining hinges.

When Neeta and Lou were finally stepping out the door, I released a breath. I'd been holding it since we'd left the staircase.

"Where the hell do you three think you're going now?" Aunt Bea's voice echoed through the foyer. "I thought we'd already settled this nonsense." Her voice was wrong somehow, as creaky as the wood floors, as whiny as the old iron door hinges.

I whirled to face her. She couldn't keep us there. We were free to leave whenever we wanted. My aunt had already said as much. But one look at Aunt Bea's face told me everything I needed to know. We weren't free, had never been. We'd been prisoners in that school as much as if we'd been inmates in a jail.

"Aunt Bea, we're leaving." I kept my voice as calm as possible. I'd already lost my parents, was I now burning another bridge? Strange or not, this woman was still my family, still my aunt.

"You're not going anywhere, none of you are. You haven't finished your training." Aunt Bea's hair was wild, more so than usual as if she hadn't brushed it in days. There was a crazed look in her eyes. She appeared more animal than human.

"Auntie." I tried employing a tactic that had worked previously. The term had always melted my aunt's heart. "Auntie, we have to go, we can't stay here anymore when so many people are in danger. I'm sorry, but we are leaving. Please don't be upset." I kept my voice soft, low enough to hopefully elicit calm.

Aunt Bea's expression did not change. There was no softening of her countenance or relaxing of her posture at being called *Auntie* by her only niece. There was only the feral glow in her eyes, a glow that began to increasingly alarm me the longer I stared.

"You're not leaving. None of you can leave." Aunt Bea planted her feet, bending slightly at the knees as if having thoughts of attacking us.

I was so shocked by what was happening that I

could only stare at her. My mouth gaped open, my eyes wide with surprise. This was not my Aunt Bea. This was not my aunt whose warmth used to spread from her eyes to her arms as she held them out to embrace me, stroking my hair as she rested her chin on the top of my head. This was not my aunt who gave me naughty books to read when I was probably a little too young to read them. This was not my aunt who I always trusted implicitly and who was fun, kind, and honest.

Just when I thought the scene could not get any weirder, Aunt Bea held out a hand, her blue light flickering to life in the palm she held outstretched. She was going to attack us.

I snapped my mouth closed.

"I don't want to hurt you, but I will do what I must to keep you under this roof." Aunt Bea's face glowed behind her light, her eyes all the more terrifying.

"We don't have time for this. Miranda, step aside." Neeta's voice, not soft and calming but loud and commanding, echoed through the foyer.

I did as I was told, stepping back into the still open doorway, Billie, and Lou on the stoop outside. Neeta edged her way around me, one hand shoved in the pocket of her shorts, the other hand held out in front of her just as Aunt Bea's was. In her pocket, I knew Neeta was grasping her touchstone, her bit of red sandstone she'd found and practiced with in the garden. Neeta's power came to life in her hand as a small ball of blue flame. Now that Neeta had control, she could choose the level of power she hurled at someone or something, and I knew she would choose a level that was likely to hurt but not kill my aunt.

For one mad second, I considered shoving Neeta aside rather than allowing her to knock Aunt Bea off her feet. But there was no stopping this now. We had to leave. In order for that to happen, Aunt Bea had to be held off so we could run.

With sadness in my eyes, I took a firmer hold of my suitcase. We were about to run, and we were about to run fast. I could already hear Billie and Lou behind me, their footsteps edging down the steps and onto the gravel of the drive. It was best to be spaced out when it was time to flee so we weren't knocking into each other like bowling pins.

As I watched Aunt Bea over Neeta's shoulder, I noticed my aunt's eyes change. Something was dawning on her as she watched the light dance in Neeta's palm.

"For a novice such as yourself, control is best mastered through the use of a touchstone. But you wouldn't know this unless you'd read the second lesson from my grimoire." Anger suffused her face, the glow of blue from her own light turning purple as her gaze shifted from Neeta to me. "You little thief. You did read my book that night. I should have known. Your parents never trusted you. They barely even liked you. I suppose they knew more about your character than I wanted to believe."

The words were like a blow to the abdomen. I nearly doubled over from the vitriol my aunt spewed. The wind seemed to be knocked from me, pain seeping into my chest as I gulped for a breath of air. My eyes stung with tears. My aunt had dealt me a final blow, the last member of my family to cut me to the quick.

"Enough of this." As Neeta said the last word, she unleashed her light toward Aunt Bea. Since her attention was on me, she didn't see it coming until it was too late.

Aunt Bea tried dodging the blast, unleashing her own power as she dove to the side, only she didn't react in time. As Aunt Bea took her dive, Neeta's blast hit her in the shoulder, propelling her backward against the solid wood railing of the staircase. She hit the side of her head as she fell in a heap onto the floor. The blast Aunt Bea had managed to release hit the window alongside the door, exploding the pane in a shower of glass shards.

Neeta and I ducked. I dropped my suitcase to cover my face with my hands.

When the glass had settled, Neeta jumped up. "Bill!" she yelled out.

"We're fine," Billie called out from the drive. "Not even a scratch."

Me and Neeta had not been so lucky. I felt warmth on my forehead. I reached up to touch a tender cut on the top of my head.

"Let me look." Neeta pushed my head down, her fingers exploring my scalp.

I winced.

"It's small." Neeta released me. "Bill, we need tissues."

I glanced up as Billie edged around me back into the foyer. She glanced at the crumpled body of Aunt Bea before running down the hall to the kitchen.

"You're cut, too." Lou appeared at my shoulder, then moved by me to spin Neeta around. Lou held her hand over a small cut on Neeta's neck. "I don't think it'll need stitches."

Coming back to my senses, I rushed past them, my shoes crunching glass. From a distance, Aunt Bea looked sickeningly twisted, but when I reached her, I realized my aunt was all in one piece. Nothing appeared broken. She had a knot on the side of her head and was knocked out cold, but she was breathing and appeared otherwise unscathed.

"Is she alive?" Neeta asked behind me.

"Yeah, she'll probably be fine." I crouched alongside my aunt, the wildness of her previous appearance tempered in her sleep.

"I'm sorry, Miranda. I didn't want to hurt her, but we had to stop her."

Billie rushed back onto the scene, a wad of paper towels in one hand, a first aid kit in the other.

"It's fine. Your blast was a small one. Hers was meant to do serious harm." This was hard for me to say out loud, but it was true. The blast Aunt Bea had sent hurtling toward the window could have killed any one of us.

Billie opened the first aid kit, but before she could nurse anyone, Lou spoke up. "We need to get going. We can doctor wounds in the car. Who knows how long she'll be out."

Billie snapped the kit shut, handing a paper towel to me then Neeta. We applied pressure to our cuts, regathered our things, then left the school, one by one. I was the last to exit. I closed the heavy door behind me with one last look back at my aunt, still on the ground in what seemed a peaceful sleep. The shattered window was a gaping wound in the front of the beautiful, old building.

The car wasn't far. We walked quickly but didn't run. I pressed the paper towel to my head, my suitcase in one hand. Lou had taken the quilt from me, slinging it over her shoulder.

No one spoke until we were inside the car. Lou offered to drive first so Billie could help tend to wounds. Neeta sat in the front passenger seat, her neck easily accessible to Billie who sat right behind her.

I slumped against the seat beside Billie, watching her as she cleaned and then covered Neeta's cut with a sterile pad and tape. As she worked, I was reminded of Billie's dream of being a nurse. Billie had confessed this to me when we'd first met not all that long ago. Her job as a sex worker was going to lead her to nursing school, that was her goal. I had been so touched by this confession at the time. I'd been so shocked by what Billie did for a living, but once I'd gotten to know her, I'd realized that Billie was a person with hopes and dreams just like anyone else.

Once everyone had been doctored, we settled in for the long ride. Lou had managed to grab several snacks from the kitchen in a short amount of time. The reusable grocery bag contained a bunch of bananas, an almost full loaf of bread, a brand-new jar of peanut butter, crackers, and six apples. At least we wouldn't starve.

Billie passed out a banana each to serve as breakfast. As she peeled hers back, she glanced over at me. "Do you want to talk about what happened, honey?"

I shook my head, my mouth half full of sticky banana. "Not really," I mumbled before swallowing. "What is there to say anyway? My family sucks? Believe me, I got the message loud and clear. Not a mistake I'll ever make again."

"Something was off about Bea, that wasn't her." Lou was pulling onto the main road that would take us to the highway we'd travel all the way to El Paso, Texas.

"I agree." Neeta craned her neck as best she could to look at me. "The lady I met at the Stanley Hotel was not the same lady of the past two days. It was almost like she was deteriorating before our eyes. She went from sweet and normal, to odd, to downright terrifying."

"Why, though?" Billie asked. "What could have caused the change?"

"You don't think it was something magical, do you?" Lou pulled into traffic. "Something new we have to worry about?"

"Oh, god." Billie laid her half-eaten banana in her lap. "Like, magical powers can make us crazy? All we need is more shit to worry about."

"I don't think that was it." I pulled the quilt over my lap. I needed the comfort. "But whatever it was, I agree, something was affecting her."

"Well, whatever it was," Neeta said from the front seat, "let's worry about one thing at a time. I don't mean to be insensitive, Miranda, but we have to focus on what comes next."

"Agreed." I pulled the quilt tighter.

Neeta sighed. "What we need to do now is talk about where we're going, then resume our reading of the grimoire."

Lou's head snapped to the side. "You have the grimoire? Bea's grimoire?"

"We do, and we'll share the knowledge with you and everyone else. This isn't stuff that should be kept a secret. This is information every witch needs."

"Exactly." Billie resumed eating her banana. "As for where we go, that seems obvious. We go to the Trumpet."

"What about Ruby's? That seems the obvious choice to me." I rolled my head, resting against the back of the seat toward Billie.

"Only Ruby's is where Ash was picked up, it's where you and Neeta worked. It seems logical that whoever *they* are, they'll be watching that club like hawks. Not only that, but Joey knows where Ash is, and it's probably a safe bet that wherever Ash is, Crystal is probably near."

Neeta's head bobbed up and down. "The Trumpet it is."

Chapter Thirteen

We drove straight through. For eleven hours, we drove through the cities of northern Colorado, the plains of southern Colorado, a mountain pass, more plains, some desert, or at least that's what Billie called New Mexico, before we arrived in Dallas, Texas. The clock on the dash read 8 PM, and we had at least eight more hours to go. The car was not as old as I imagined it was. The black VW Jetta was probably a late 90s model. The mileage was low, and the car was in great shape, as if it hadn't been driven much.

The time spent driving had been used to read through the grimoire, Neeta and Billie taking turns at the wheel with Lou. Four more lessons had been uncovered—we'd skipped over ones that didn't seem important to the task at hand such as brewing potions for different types of ailments, focusing on what we needed to free our friends and fight the forces that be. We'd learned more about grounding ourselves while casting our power, a summoning spell, which taught us how to summon a spirit to do your bidding, how to heal minor wounds with our light, and most interesting of all, how to throw up a shield of defense.

As we stopped at a gas station to fill up the Jetta's tank, which had weathered all the driving surprisingly well, we took turns going two at a time to the bathroom which thankfully was located outside and around the back of the gas station. Lou went inside to pay and buy snacks and drinks. The rest of us were still wanted after all. Our money situation was becoming critical, but we were almost there.

We were back on our way in less than fifteen minutes with me now in the driver's seat. I would drive the next four hours while the others tried sleeping. Then I'd switch with Neeta who wanted to be the one to take us into New Orleans while I attempted to snooze for the remainder of the drive.

The fact that we'd all be tired by the time we arrived was not worth discussing. This was the path we were on now, and there was no stopping.

Exactly four hours after I started driving, I pulled over. We were not quite to Alexandria, Louisiana, the vegetation lush on either side of the car as we were heading into swamp country.

Neeta walked around to the driver's side while I crawled over the console, buckling myself in and snuggling into the quilt the best I could. Resting for the next few hours would be vital. No one knew what awaited us. We had no idea if we'd have to jump right into fighting or if we'd be able to get some sleep before the action.

Another possibility was getting pulled over, but we hadn't come across a single police car or roadblock, the highways were mostly deserted like a scene from *The Walking Dead* but without all the abandoned vehicles.

I nodded off while Neeta drove, the glass from the window cold against the side of my head. Before I knew what was happening, I woke with a start. Blinking through bleary eyes, I could see the car had come to a stop. Did we make it?

"We're here, ya'll." Neeta poked my thigh through the quilt, her voice loud and sure.

I sat up, my neck aching from the odd angle at which I'd slept. Behind me, I heard the others coming to life.

We were there, all right. As my vision cleared, I saw we were in a parking lot on the edge of the Quarter. The sun was fully up at almost seven in the morning, illuminating the old-world buildings, the wrought iron railings I loved.

I looked around before opening the door, stepping into the already warm day. My sneakers hit pavement and I inhaled the close, humid air around me. I'd missed this. I'd missed this place so much. After being gone less than a week, there was no denying it—New Orleans felt like home in a way home never did.

"We're only two blocks from the Trumpet and Joey's apartment." Billie was getting out of the back of the car, her bag already slung over a shoulder.

"I know." Neeta too was stretching her back on the opposite side of the car. "We need to figure out what we're doing with this car. Should we ditch it here or somewhere safer, or should we try and keep it? Miranda, do you think Bea will report it missing?"

"Probably, that sort of behavior seems to track for my family."

"Then this is what we should do." Neeta closed the door. "We go to Joey's, get an update on the situation, then have him bring us back here. He can follow us in his truck so we can ditch the car in the swamp. Then we'll go from there."

"We go to the Trumpet, not his apartment. We go in through the back, remember, there's no cameras there." Billie was bouncing, ready to run the two blocks to Joey.

"It's early, will he be there? And how do we know his phone wasn't being monitored?" Lou was asking the important questions, her tote bag swinging in her hand.

"He'll be there. And he had a burner phone, remember? He gave me the number before we left."

"I like Joey more and more all the time. Make sure we have everything in case we can't come back for the car." Neeta pulled out her backpack, slamming the door closed after.

I stuck my head back in to grab the quilt then went around to the back for my suitcase.

"Won't we look weird, walking through the French Quarter with our belongings?" Lou looked around us warily.

"Too early," Billie answered. "Even before all the weirdness, no one was up before noon in the Quarter."

"Yeah," Neeta echoed. "Besides, four women walking through the Quarter with their possessions is probably the least weird thing anyone here will see all day."

Lou chuckled, both hands in front of her holding the handle of her bag. "If you say so."

I hadn't thought to ask Lou if she'd ever been to New Orleans before. I thought back to the first time I'd walked through the Quarter, in awe of not only the from-another-time beauty but also the uniqueness, the otherness that made New Orleans so special. I felt a little sheepish for a moment as I realized I really knew nothing about Lou. Was she even from Colorado? What was her home life like? Was she without family like I was? The ride from Estes Park had been devoted to study of the grimoire and rest, but I found myself wishing I'd taken a few minutes to get to know her better.

"Come on." Billie wasn't willing to wait any longer. She started walking toward the street. "We'll take the alley behind Chartres, then we only have to be on Canal for a few minutes."

"No one knows their way around the Quarter better than Billie," Neeta said as she took up the rear.

This was normally a joke Billie would laugh at, but she was too focused. Only two blocks and about ten minutes separated her and Joey, and she couldn't spare a single thought for anything else. I envied my friend as I followed her up Canal, then down the sour smelling alley. There was no telling how long it would be before I saw Ash again. It was hard to admit that there was a small irritating fear in the back of my mind that made me wonder if I'd ever see her, at all. That fear had been present the moment we parted and had never left.

Where the streets of New Orleans were charming, the alleys were not. The backs of the buildings were in some disrepair, bricks appearing on the verge of crumbling in some places. Little black cockroaches skittered from time to time with the fall of one foot or another. Trash day must be soon because bins were teetering with foul smelling refuse.

"This is disgusting." Lou walked behind me, her small feet stepping daintily over puddles of unidentifiable sludge.

"Almost there." The excitement in Billie's voice was audible, her words almost a squeal.

The alley was beginning to look familiar. That night not long ago when Neeta's powers came to the fore in a fantastic display of fireworks inside the Trumpet leapt to my mind. The looks on the faces of the bikers playing pool, how the shock registered in the widening of their eyes, the gaping of their mouths. They'd run out of the joint hell bent on calling the law, but Joey had saved the day. He'd saved us.

Who would have thought a quiet, unassuming bartender would have held such depths? Billie knew. She'd known from the start.

The back door of the Trumpet materialized ahead of us. Billie broke into an all-out run, almost colliding with the closed door.

She held one hand over the knob, turning back with tear-filled eyes. "I didn't even think to make myself up. Do I look like shit?" She blinked her eyes at me.

"You've never looked like shit a single day that I've known you. Joey is going to fall over when he sees you." I wasn't lying. Billie was the beauty of the group. Her short, blonde hair may have been a little smashed from sleeping in the car, her porcelain skin a little on the pallid side with nothing to color her cheeks, but she looked far younger than her twenty-three years, fresh faced and ready to see her love.

She nodded, taking in my compliments, then wrenched open the door.

The barrel of a shotgun greeted her.

Billie jumped back, nearly knocking me on my ass.

"Oh, Christ. Billie." Joey filled the doorway, the top of his head nearly grazing the frame. He set down the rifle, butt first, leaning it against a wall, before stepping out the back and scooping Billie up in his arms. "I'm so sorry," he breathed. "I thought it would take you days to get back." He held her tight, his open flannel shirt twisted up his sides. He looked about as rough as the rest of us, his hair in desperate need of a trim, an almost full beard on his chin and cheeks.

"What is this?" Billie pulled back, her hand playing with the fluff on his face.

"I haven't really had time for grooming lately." He stepped aside, ushering her in through the open back door. "Go in. Miranda, Neeta." He pulled me into a hug, holding out a hand for Neeta who stood behind Lou. She joined the hug, but only for a quick second.

"Is anyone in there?" she asked.

"No. I haven't been open for a few days, not since, well, not since Crystal and Ash."

Neeta swallowed. I understood what she was doing. She, too had to swallow her pain. We had other more pressing matters. Falling apart was not on the table.

Neeta inclined her head toward Lou. "This is Lou, a new friend from Colorado. We have a lot to talk about."

Joey nodded, nudging them all through the door. "Coffee's on."

We sat around the half-moon table where Neeta's powers had come to life. Not thinking about Ash and how I felt about her that night was hard, so I distracted myself with the hot coffee and fresh cheese Danishes that Joey passed around.

His coffee was good, maybe the best I had drunk outside a café—strong but not bitter, just like I liked it and needed it. I closed my eyes, inhaling the scent, yearning for better days.

Neeta, Lou, and I all sat on the banquette. Joey and Billie sat side by side on bar stools in front of us. They hadn't let go of each other since we'd all been locked inside. Now they sat, holding hands, while Joey recounted the events of the past days.

"Things are getting weirder, that's for sure. Right after you guys left, the city seemed to become a ghost town. There are still some locals about, you can't keep bayou folk in their homes for long, but there aren't any tourists. Most of the gift shops and restaurants are closed, with only a handful of bars still operating. I decided to close temporarily. There's not much money coming in anyway."

"What happened to my mom?" Neeta was pinching the skin of her arm, a toe tapping under the table.

I understood how she felt as I, too, was itching to get to the heart of the matter. Where were our loved ones?

Joey nodded, his gaze softening as he looked at

Neeta. "I only know what happened to Crystal secondhand, actually thirdhand. I heard through Ruby, when I went to the club to check on the others, and Ruby heard it from your dad who was there when she was taken."

Neeta's grip on her arm tightened.

Rather than allow her to rip off her skin, I laid my hand over Neeta's.

"What does my dad have to do with this?" she asked.

"Nothing, as far as I know. They were having lunch. Apparently, your dad was attempting to woo her back. They were approached by two men in gray suits and sunglasses. One of the men showed your mom a photo of you and asked her to identify you. According to Ruby, she refused to answer, told them to leave. Your dad backed her up, asked the men to identify themselves and which organization they worked for. They didn't even acknowledge him. At that point, one of the men pulled out a pair of handcuffs and told Crystal she was being arrested for failing to provide information. Your dad jumped out of his seat to stand between Crystal and the men. It was then that several uniformed police officers entered the restaurant, restraining your dad while Crystal was drug out. Your dad did everything he could, or so I was told. He tried his best to reason with the men, to get information on where they were taking her. They told him because she wasn't a minor and because there was a special precedent for public safety, they did not have to disclose anything."

Neeta sank back against the hard seat of the banquette, my hand still over hers.

"What about Ash?" I was afraid to hear what Joey had to say, but at least I knew he had a location.

"I was sitting with Ruby at the bar while she told

me about Crystal. Ash was behind the bar drying glasses, listening to us, but not. She appeared like she was in a bit of a daze. I told Ruby I was worried about them, all of them, in light of what was happening, and maybe she should close the club for a while, maybe we could come up with some sort of plan. Before Ruby could even respond to me, the doors burst open and in came two men in gray suits. It was as if all the air had been sucked out of the place. We were silent, watching them walk toward us like maybe they weren't real, like maybe it wasn't really happening. I heard a glass shatter. Looking toward Ash, I realized she had dropped the glass she was drying. She was as rigid as me and Ruby. They went right for her, Miranda. They knew who they wanted, and they wanted Ash. Didn't even bother asking Ruby or me any questions. One of the guys went around the bar. He grabbed Ash by her arm and yanked her out. Ruby and I stood, but at that moment, it was like *The Matrix*, just as your dad had described to Ruby. A group of uniformed officers rushed in, positioning themselves between us and her. I remembered what your dad said about Crystal not being a minor, so I yelled out to the nearest gray-suited asshole that I was Ash's uncle and I demanded to know where they were taking her, that she was a minor. Without saying a word, he handed me a card and they were gone."

My mouth had gone dry. The world had become something out of a movie. This wasn't real. It couldn't be. Maybe I was in a coma in a hospital bed in Colorado having dreamt all of this up—witches, strange men in gray suits, women taken to secret locations. How could this be life?

"Where is the card?" I managed to say.

Joey leaned forward, the hand not entwined with Billie's digging into his back pocket. He placed the card on the table, pushing it toward me.

The business-sized card was basic white.

1825 Navigation Rd, New Orleans La
Temporary Holding Facility
M-F 8am-3pm

No one touched the card, but we all leaned forward to take a look.

Billie was the first to speak. "What a strange thing. To actually hand out a card with the address of the facility."

"And only to families of women who are minors." I took a deep breath.

"What do you want to bet they aren't there long enough for family members to do anything about it." Lou cupped her chin in the palm of her hand as she stared at the card.

I wanted to scream. Instead, I said, in as calm a voice as I could, "At least it's a place to start."

"Yeah," Billie echoed. "If it wasn't for Joey's quick thinking, we wouldn't even have this."

She was right. Joey had given us a starting place, the ability to begin the game on square one. This was far better than nothing.

"True, Billie." Neeta looked up at Joey, her face softening a bit. "We wouldn't have had a clue where to start without this. Thank you, Joey. Thank you for being someone we can rely on. You have no idea how precious that is these days."

Joey looked down at his lap as if the praise embarrassed him. "I'd like to think there are more people like me out there. Maybe they're scared and don't know what to do, or maybe there are more people working behind the scenes. It's hard for us to know."

"The real question" —Lou slid her elbow off the table— "is what do we do now? Do we really think we're ready to walk into some government facility and start blasting people?"

"Being ready is beside the point." I picked up the card, turning it over in my hand.

****

Being ready *was* beside the point. We were going to that facility, and we were going today. The women who were shuffled through there wouldn't stay for long. Every minute we wasted was a minute we could miss Ash, Crystal, or both.

After Lou's initial reticence, she now seemed completely on board. The four of us took turns in the dingy bathroom behind the jukebox, tying back hair, changing into functional clothing, and splashing water on our faces.

Neeta and I stood by the front doors, peering out through the blinds at the mostly deserted streets.

"We'll take the car to the facility. Joey will follow in his truck. Hopefully, we'll get out Ash and Mom, and as many others as we can."

I was nodding. In my mind I was already there, already pulling Ash out of a cell.

"What do you want to do about the grimoire?"

"What do you mean?" I glanced at her then.

"We should bring it with us, right? We can't risk leaving it here. What if something happens and we can't return?" Neeta made sense. The smartest course of action would be to take the pages of the grimoire.

"It will be hard for me to stuff all of it in my pockets. We'll have to divide it up. Or we could give it to Joey to hold onto since he'll be right behind us." We needed our hands free and carrying around loose pages of a book that meant life or death to us would be difficult.

Lou joined us at the window. "Dividing up the pages would be best. That way, if we need to find a spell in an emergency, the grimoire is on us."

"Lou makes a good point." Neeta leaned against the blinds, the sections snapping against her shoulder. "I feel confident we have all we need to get in and out quickly, but we should prepare for all possible scenarios. If we get trapped, the book will come in handy."

"Okay," I agreed. "We each carry a fourth in our pockets. Just be careful. We can't afford to lose any of it."

I went over to my suitcase, resting on the bar top. I popped it open, pulling out the pages of the grimoire from the interior pocket. The pages were divided equally into four parts and handed out. I divided my portion into two, then folded the pages the best I could before sinking each wad into each of my front pockets. Neeta, Billie, and Lou did the same.

"What do I do?" Joey stood back, watching us tuck away the papers. "I can back you up with the rifle."

"We don't want to kill anyone, do we?" I felt squeamish around guns as it was. The thought of shooting strangers, even if they were a threat, made me nauseous.

"We're going to do our best not to. I think something we want to prove is that we aren't dangerous. We aren't going to go around killing people just because we can. We'll do our best to stun only." Neeta smiled at Joey. "The sentiment is a nice one, Joey. Thank you again for being willing to protect us, but I think it best you stay in your truck with the engine running. The most important thing you can do for us is get people out."

Joey looked at Billie. "But then I can't keep tabs on what's happening inside."

Billie moved to him, taking his hand in both of hers. "I'll be okay. Promise. I've learned a lot in the last few days." She glanced at the others. "We all have."

A loud knock on the back door made me jump.

"Who the hell is that?"

"I'll check." Joey rushed to the door, snatching up his rifle from the wall. He opened a peephole I had not seen before and looked out. He fumbled with the lock, opening the latch and pushing the door wide.

Ruby rushed in. Her eyes were wide in her haste, but the rest of her was as perfectly put together as always. She wore a brunette wig, a little on the demure side for Ruby, a black jumpsuit clinging to every padded curve. She threw open her arms. "There's my girls."

I ran, almost headfirst into Ruby's soft shoulder, Neeta and Billie crowding me for space inside Ruby's embrace. She smelled like softly scented floral perfume. I closed my eyes to take it all in.

"Lord, I was worried about the three of you." Ruby enfolded us all in her arms the best she could. "Who's your friend?"

Neeta was the first to step back. "Lou, this is Ruby. Ruby, Lou."

"Nice to meet you, Lou." Ruby surveyed the room, her arms now empty. "So, what are we doing?"

Neeta laughed. "There's no beating around the bush with Ruby."

"No, ma'am, so tell me, what are we cooking?"

I felt suddenly cold outside of Ruby's warm embrace. I crossed my arms around myself. "We've learned some good spells over the last few days, as well as how to control our powers better."

Ruby raised an eyebrow but didn't interrupt, so I continued. "We're going to the facility, the place on the card that the man in the gray suit gave Joey. And actually, your appearance could not have come at a better time."

"Why is that?"

"You can drive a second getaway car."

Neeta huffed behind her. "I don't like putting this many people in danger. I was already leery about Joey, but now Ruby, too? We have too many other things to worry about. We can't be worried about protecting everyone."

"Neeta." Ruby leveled Neeta with one glare. "I don't need anybody to be worried about me. I can take of myself, and I know for a fact that young man" —she pointed at Joey— "can take of himself."

"Exactly." Joey stepped up alongside Ruby. "The least we can do is drive."

Chapter Fourteen

The address on the card took us to the very edge of town. This area was mostly swampland, more and more of the land mass being taken over by water.

"Are you sure we're going in the right direction?" Lou sat in the passenger's seat, in front of me. Her head looked out the window, turning every which way as she took in the scenery. I was pretty sure Lou had never seen a swamp before.

"This is right. I know this area." Neeta leaned forward from the middle seat as Ruby drove slowly down the deserted dirt road. "There used to be a school out here. My parents went there."

Ruby pumped the brakes hard, everyone in the car jerking forward. "I'm guessing that's it."

Billie unbuckled her seatbelt, wriggling forward in the seat. "Pull off the road before they see us."

Neeta had the better vantage point. I tried peering around the seat in front of me. "What is it? I can't see." I tried craning my head around Neeta's broad shoulder but didn't see a thing as Ruby pulled off onto the shoulder and a little way into the trees.

Joey pulled in behind her. He remained in his car.

Ruby cut the engine.

Neeta explained what she was seeing. "A tall gate, pointed at the top, so no way to climb over. We'll have to go through it."

"Did you see anyone? I didn't." Billie looked out the rear window, a wan smile on her lips for Joey.

"I think there was a guard station off to the right." Lou put her hand on the door handle.

"Okay," Neeta said. "Three of us takes out the guards, one of us opens the gate."

"*Takes out.* That makes me nervous." Billie pressed her forehead against the back of Ruby's seat.

"Me too, Bill. We just have to remember our training. We have to focus, stay grounded, and in control. The three of us have our touchstones and have had some practice, so I think Lou should be the one to open the gate." Neeta glanced over at Lou. "Can you do that?"

She nodded. "Easy." They'd given Lou a crash course on control and finding your centering object, but there'd been no time to actually let her find one.

"This is it, ladies." Neeta looked back and forth from me to Billie. "Can you believe this is where we are?" She huffed a little laugh.

"No." I couldn't believe it. Another surreal feeling came over me like I was watching a movie starring myself. How could this be real life?

"We stick to the trees and only come out when we're ready to blast them, nicely blast them. Remember we only want to stun these people, knock them out. Focus on that thought while you're summoning your power." Neeta opened her car door. "Let's go."

We all stepped out simultaneously. Before moving forward, we all took a moment to take stock of the surroundings. There was an earthy wetness in the air. All was silent. Without looking behind us at our friends, we crept into the forest.

The guard house was inside the fence, next to the gate. We weren't far from the gate which made me wonder if we'd been seen or heard, but the closer we crept, the more I could see that all seemed normal at the guard house. Two men, both in camouflage jumpsuits with rifle straps across their chests, stood outside smoking cigarettes. One man, tall and razor thin, had his foot up on the stump of a tree, the cigarette dangling from his mouth at a dangerous angle. The other was average looking with a big, bushy beard that reminded me of Trapper, his cigarette held aloft between his fingers. The men were having an animated conversation, which may have been why they were oblivious to the cars coming down the road.

I thought my heart may actually beat its way free of my chest. My hands shook as I quickly became sweaty all over. Wiping my palms on my pants, I did my best to dry them before the assault. I wasn't sure what moisture would do to my light ball, and I didn't want to find out.

Neeta led the way as usual, me mostly alongside her. Billie and Lou were behind us.

Neeta crouched down behind a row of hedges right in front of the fence. The guards, had they been paying any attention at all, should have seen us. She nodded once to me. This was our cue to start warming up.

I inhaled one long breath, held it, then concentrated all my thoughts and feelings on the power. I closed my eyes, imagining Ash on the other side of the fence, scared and alone inside a cell with no hope of escape. I let this feeling of fear, of isolation, wash over me, accepting my own feelings of terror at never seeing Ash again. The grimoire was right, the feelings fueled the power. My hand warmed, my breath centering. When I knew I was ready, I opened my eyes. Together, we rose to our feet.

The guards, still arguing over some mundane issue, took a beat too long to notice us. With Billie stepping alongside me, all three of us stood together, backs straight, dancing balls of light bouncing in the palms of our outstretched hands. Billie would hold hers unless needed.

The men threw down their cigarettes, but they were too late. Me and Neeta had already unleashed our power, holding back our full force. The twin balls of blue light hit one man in his cheek, then the other one straight in the middle of his forehead. They were knocked backward as if hit by a truck. They fell back, each looking like a crumpled scarecrow falling off his cross. I worried they were dead, but there was no way to check just yet.

The second we unleashed our blasts, Lou jumped into the road, sending her own blast at the center of the gate. The effect was a loud crunch of metal on metal as the light hit the lock, busting the gates wide. Sneaking in was now out of the question. They knew we were coming. My stomach fell into my toes.

We didn't hesitate. Lou ran in first, dashing to the guards to check for a pulse.

Billie, her light still visible in her palm, swore in Lou's direction. "We don't have time for that."

"I had to make sure." Lou rejoined them. "I'm going to stay here as a distraction. Go."

There wasn't time to argue. We ran, full tilt, around the back of the building.

The plan was to enter the rear if we were found out. All of us, together. The army would rush out the front to confront us, hopefully leaving the rear unguarded and easily accessible. At no point were we to become separated, this would only make us vulnerable. But there hadn't been time to think, only act.

I was starting to get tired of Neeta always taking the lead, so I pushed ahead, staying close to the building, edging my shoulder around corners. I was beginning to feel more and more anxious for Ash. Getting to her was the only thing on my mind.

"Stay smart," Neeta said behind me like she could read my mind. I knew Neeta was just as anxious over Crystal.

Gunshots sounded behind us, toward the front of

the building. I hesitated for a second, Neeta pressing me on with a gentle hand. Still, I glanced behind me as if I could see what was happening. I couldn't.

Neeta nudged me again. "We can't stop, not now. All this would have been for nothing."

"But Lou." I continued around the next corner, more slowly this time.

"Lou chose to stay behind."

Neeta was right; she did choose. Somehow, that simple fact didn't make me feel any better.

We had edged around the last corner. The back of the property was deserted, an old playground. Swings hanging by one chain swung in a phantom wind. The teeter-totter on its side loomed ahead, another haunting display of abandonment.

"I thought this was the school, but the front looked different, and the gate was definitely new. How weird that they brought my mom to be locked up in her old elementary school."

"What is it with creepy old schools?" Billie whispered behind us.

I turned so we were in a sort of a huddle. Mayhem seemed to be erupting at the front of the grounds. There was so much shouting, but we had to remain focused on the task at hand. I looked to Neeta to tell us what to do. I may have wanted to lead us to this point, but Neeta was the one who always came up with the plans.

Neeta chewed on her lower lip. "We have to work fast," she said. "Once we get into the back door, we take a quick survey of the layout. Where there are guards, there will be prisoners. We do not hesitate. Blast anyone in your way. We'll have to stay focused, keep reloading, as it were, as we move. If you can't keep your light going, fall back. Okay?" She looked at each of us in turn.

I nodded.

Billie closed her eyes but nodded too.

Neeta reached out both her hands, taking our arms. "I love you two. Please don't die."

Billie opened her eyes, a slight chuckle moving past her lips. "Same."

I tried not to feel the tightening of my throat. "Same."

I pressed Neeta ahead, and we moved toward the back door. It was locked.

Neeta covered the knob with her hand, sending a surge of blue light through the mechanism. It clicked open.

"Killer," Billie whispered.

We went in. We entered a workroom. There was a long metal desk, some rusted filing cabinets, and a big white-faced clock on the wall. A smell of old ink, probably from the massive printer, filled the air.

Neeta went to the door, pressing her ear to the crack. She must have been confident, because she turned the knob, sending us out into a hallway, the avocado green linoleum under our feet worn almost to the subfloor.

We stopped to listen. From inside we could hear none of the chaos outside. The hallway ran in two directions from where we stood. One side was completely dark, the other lighted way down at the end.

Without acknowledging what we were doing, we moved side by side by side in the direction of the light. The fluorescents zinged overhead, flickering as we walked.

Before we reached the end, we heard voices. Whoever was speaking was male and was keeping their voice low. He was right around the corner.

I stuck my hand in my pocket, cradling the piece of petrified wood. My right hand sparked to life. This was it; we were out of time. Without even surveying the situation, we stepped around the corner, hands alight.

Three men stood in front of a set of closed double doors. One man wore a gray suit. The other two wore camo jumpsuits, their scary looking guns in their hands, pointing right at me and Billie.

The man in the gray suit laughed. "You three must think we're idiots. The card I gave your boyfriend?" He leveled a glare toward Billie. "Did you really think it would lead to your friends? There are only three idiots here, and I'm looking at them. Put down your hands, and no one will get hurt. We already have your little pink haired girl out front."

"Shit," Neeta said under her breath.

"Yeah, I'd say you're in some shit." The man in the gray suit smiled a crooked smile, his eyes hidden behind dark glasses.

Once Neeta dropped her hand, Billie followed suit. I closed my palm into a fist but didn't drop it. We couldn't give up; we couldn't surrender. If we didn't fight our way out of this, no matter the cost, who knew where we would end up, what would happen to us. We were the only ones, besides Aunt Bea and Sara, who had training in the grimoire, and something was wrong with Aunt Bea. If we disappeared, who was left to save us?

One of the spells from the grimoire leapt to mind. On the drive from Estes Park, we'd read about summoning spirits. A spirit could be summoned to perform all manner of tasks, the most useful of which in the current situation was to hold or bind an enemy.

The man in the gray suit didn't appear to have a weapon, at least not anything he could access quickly. If I took a step back, I could blast both the guards with one shot, then summon the spirit. It was a shot in the dark, but one I knew I had to take.

With my heart racing in my chest, I took one quick jump backward. The plan was in motion. I threw out my hand, the blue light hitting the men with more force than I'd intended. They flew back, hitting the wall behind them and crumpling to the ground.

Mr. Gray Suit reached around his back, probably to grab a gun in the waistband of his pants.

"Hold him!" I screamed at Billie and Neeta.

Neither hesitated, rushing Gray Suit and pinning him between them, his arms immobile.

"What are you doing?" Neeta asked, her arms like vise grips on her hostage as he fought them with everything he had.

"Summoning a spirit." I closed my eyes, concentrating every ounce of my brainpower on the chant from the spell book. Light danced in my upturned palm as I repeated the phrase, out loud, over and over.

Spirits of the dead, heed my call
Spirits of the dead, bind this man
Spirits of the dead, heed my call
Spirits of the dead, bind this man
Spirits of the dead, heed my call
Spirits of the dead, bind this man

The man squirmed. He bucked against Neeta and Billie, shouting for help as loud as he could. His mouth couldn't be covered while they were holding him, so I had to work fast.

After I repeated the phrase for the seventh time, my arm vibrated in a way it never had before. This magic was new to me. I couldn't break my concentration.

Focus, Miranda. Ride it out.

I did. I rode the wave of the vibrations. When Billie gasped, I opened my eyes. There in front of me, standing between me and my friends, was a shimmery apparition. The spirit had no form, no face. I pointed at the man, held suspended between Neeta and Billie.

The ball of light, my witch's power, melted into string, intertwining with my fingers. "Hold him. Cover his mouth."

The formless shape moved over the man who went rigid underneath the shimmering veil.

Neeta and Billie stepped away.

"Woah," Billie said.

"Follow us," I said to the spirit.

The gray suited man had gone silent and immobile.

"Come on," I said to my friends. "Let's get out of here before we lose our chance."

Without giving them time to argue or even talk, I took off back down the hallway. Neeta and Billie ran alongside me. With one quick glance over my shoulder, I saw the man running behind us, his face completely blank of all emotion.

I knew I wouldn't be able to hold the spirit for long. The grimoire said the spell was temporary, at the most lasting an hour. I hoped this would be long enough to get the guy back to the Trumpet where we could make him tell us where Ash and Crystal were.

"We'll have to exit the property somewhere else, then circle back. No way we can go through the front gate." Neeta huffed as she ran and talked.

We had come through the workroom to the back door. I looked at the spirit-covered man. "How do we get out of here without being caught?"

The oddly catatonic man looked at me with dead eyes. "There is a back gate, hidden amongst some giant oaks, with only one guard."

"Lead us," I said to him.

Neeta opened the door, the gray suited man sprinting away.

We followed, careful to look around as we sped through the defunct playground and across the weed-filled expanse that at one time must have been a baseball field.

The back gate was guarded by one man, just as he'd said. There was no guardhouse, just a man leaning against a post inspecting his nails.

"Everyone walks. You," I said to Gray Suit's back. "Tell him to open the gate. That we're on a special assignment." This was all I could think of at the moment, and I prayed with all my might that the words sounded official enough for the guard to let us through without incident.

"Open the gate." Gray Suit barked the words at the guard. The guard was so startled he almost dropped his gun. One look at the man who'd spoken to him sent him quivering. I prayed that the guard wouldn't see the shimmer.

"Yes, sir." The guard keyed in a number on the keypad, the gate clicking open. He held it wide for us to pass, eyeing us as we walked behind Gray Suit. "Is everything okay, sir? I thought I heard shots fired but did my job and held my post."

"We're on a special assignment." It was all Gray Suit said. He'd repeated my instructions verbatim, not able to offer any improvisation.

"Of course, sir." The guard didn't seem put off by this, which made me think the gray suits often spoke like robots.

We stepped through the gate, the guard shutting it behind us. We continued walking until we were out of sight.

I put out a hand to stop Neeta. "Okay, now we need to double back to the cars."

"They won't be there. Remember? We told Joey

and Ruby, should anything go down, they were to meet us farther down the county line road. I'd say we have quite the walk ahead of us."

Billie wasn't wrong. We were already tired and would be walking over rough terrain for some time before we reached the others.

That meant one thing—we'd have to interrogate Gray Suit now. Our spirit situation was time sensitive.

"Okay, we're going to have to get information out of this guy while we walk." I motioned with my head that Gray Suit should walk ahead of us. "We have less than an hour before we lose our control of him."

"Right." Neeta walked down the center of the path. "Where is my mom and Ash?"

Gray Suit spoke in that flat, robotic monotone. "All detainees from the southern states are being held at the old state prison outside of Shreveport, Louisiana."

Billie shot us both a wide-eyed look. I knew exactly what she meant. We could hit multiple birds with one stone.

"How many guards are at the old prison and where are they stationed?" I asked.

"Seventy-two. Half of these work the perimeter. The other half keeps the population in check."

"How are the women kept in check?" Billie failed to keep the disgust out of her voice.

"They are kept in isolation and sedated."

My blood pressure rose. Apparently, laws and rights were a thing of the past. If all the women were sedated, they would be hard to move. But that was a problem for another time. "How many detainees are there at the prison?"

"Twenty-eight."

I narrowed my eyes, shooting a quizzical look toward Neeta and Billie. They needed seventy-two guards to watch twenty-eight women. The number of women seemed low, and I was reminded of what my aunt said, there aren't as many of us as the media was making out.

"Are there any other weapons at the jail besides guns?"

"No."

"What is the plan? I mean, what does the government, or whoever, plan to do with the women?"

"They will eventually be terminated, but certain assurances have to be in place first."

"Like?"

"We have to be certain all the women have been contained. This is not only a national effort, but an international one, and not all nations are on board. Negotiations are being made."

I couldn't think of anything else to ask, and I'd had enough of the conversation.

"What else?" I asked Neeta and Billie.

Billie shook her head.

Neeta said, "Can we kill this guy?"

"No," I said. then to Gray Suit, I said, "Stop."

The man came to a dead halt.

"Turn around." This was kind of fun. I could see how summoning spirits to hold your enemies could be a power easily abused. "You will run back to the school as fast as you can. Once you get there, you will tell the others how you chased us over the fence and into the woods where you killed us and left our bodies."

"What about Lou?" Billie whispered into my ear.

I closed my eyes for a second, trying to think my way clear of a way to help Lou. Nothing leapt to mind. "We can't help her right now. If he tells them to let her go, then they'll know he isn't in his right mind. By having them hunt for our bodies in the swamp, we'll buy ourselves time to find Joey and Ruby and get the hell out of here. We'll help Lou. If we're lucky, they'll send her to the prison, and we can rescue her with everyone else. I just don't see what else we can do for her right now. Do you?"

Billie sighed, looking away at the ground. She gave a small shake of her head.

I looked at Neeta, needing her input as well. "As much as it kills me to say it, you're right. We can't do anything for her right now without sacrificing ourselves and everyone else."

I turned my attention back to Gray Suit. "Go now and do all that I've said. And thank you." I added the last part for the spirit, not Gray Suit. I'd die before I thanked him.

Gray Suit sprinted off back down the path, toward the school.

We turned, half-walking, half-jogging.

"Maybe we should have asked him who he is and who he works for." Neeta jogged and talked.

"I thought about it," I said. "But in the end decided it doesn't really matter."

"Maybe this will help." Billie pulled a black leather wallet out of her back pocket.

Neeta and I laughed.

"I stole it when the spirit took him over. Figured it wouldn't hurt to see what was inside this baby."

"Billie, you're my hero." Neeta swatted Billie's back.

She slipped the wallet back into her pocket. "We'll check it out when we get to the others. But more importantly, can we talk about how we just summoned a spirit? An honest-to-God ghost. You guys, I'm freaking out."

We laughed with Billie as we ran. I've never been much for exercise, and I certainly have never been a runner. By the time we reached the county line road, I was sweaty, my heart beating faster than it ever had in my life.

"I think I'm going to have a heart attack," I said when we finally came to a stop. I took huge gulps of air, concentrating on breathing slowly to bring down my heart rate.

"You and me both." Billie leaned over, her hands on her knees, as out of breath as I was.

"You two are wimps," Neeta said, although she too was breathing heavily. "I see the top of Joey's truck." She pointed ahead.

Billie took off at another run.

Joey must have been looking in his rearview because he hopped out of the truck and ran at her with open arms.

Neeta and I walked, side by side until we were behind them. They embraced while I did my best to swallow my bitterness. Ash should be here. I should be running into her arms. Instead, she was lying in a jail cell, all alone and drugged out of her mind. And she wasn't even a witch. Her association with all this was through me and me alone. If I'd never entered her life, she'd be living just like normal.

"Hello, Miranda?" Neeta nudged me.

"Yeah."

"Let's get out of here. I'm riding with Ruby."

Ruby sat in her car, parked ahead of Joey's truck. She started the engine, Neeta jogging to the passenger door.

I slid into the back of Joey's truck, too tired to walk the extra ten feet to Ruby's car. As we took off, I looked behind us down the deserted road. No one was there.

Chapter Fifteen

Back at the Trumpet spirits were low all around. The wallet had proved worthless. Except for the three twenties that were tucked inside, there was no ID or badge of any kind.

The guilt we all felt over losing Lou was debilitating for us all. Once we returned, Neeta went immediately to the corner booth, crossing her arms over the tabletop and laying down her head.

I sat at the bar, observing Billie sink into Joey's arms, while Ruby sidled into the booth alongside Neeta. There was so much to talk about. Joey had been brought up to speed on the car ride back, as had Ruby, but I was exhausted. Billie and Neeta had to be as well. We'd barely slept since leaving Colorado.

"I need a shower." Billie gave voice to the other thought in my head. We all needed showers.

Joey kissed the top of her golden head. "There's a room in the back with a cot and a full bath. It's bigger and cleaner than the one up here. I've been spending a lot of time here, so the cot has been handy."

"Is it safe here?" I asked. "I'm not sure we should stay."

"Where are we safe, Miranda?" Billie asked. She looked as tired as I felt. "I don't think there's anywhere we could go that they wouldn't find us eventually."

"Billie's right," Neeta said from the booth. "Let's rest, get cleaned up, then decide on our next course of action. If anything, the stunt at the school probably bought us some time. We have our powers, and Joey is armed."

Joey pointed toward the door. "We're locked in tight. Plus, with the cameras I have all over the outside,

I'll know if anyone is out there."

"Dibs on the first shower." Billie pulled away from Joey. She wasn't going to argue. I knew that Neeta was probably right, but that didn't quell all my fears. Without her usual Billie bounce, she grabbed her pink duffel from behind the bar and disappeared into the back.

Joey looked over at Neeta and Ruby. "Neeta, why don't you go nap on the cot."

Ruby shook her head at Joey. "She's already out. Snoring like a babe."

He turned his attention to me, his brown eyes were warm, kind. I understood what Billie saw in him. The man was handsome, yes, but he had depths. "Miranda, go get some sleep. I'm going to go out and get some food. Ya'll need a hot meal."

"I think I will." I was too tired to think, too tired to argue. Sleep sounded wonderful, food even better. There was a lot to plan, a lot to go over, but we were good to no one if we were dead on our feet.

"I'll keep watch over these chickens while you're gone. Make sure you lock that back door now." Ruby pulled a paperback from her handbag, leaning back into the banquette to get more comfortable.

I took a moment to study Ruby and Joey. Joey was doing this for love, Ruby for friendship. Both things I understood. But if they hadn't any ties to this madness, would they be risking their lives? It didn't take long for me to arrive at the answer—they absolutely would be. These were the kind of people who would always stand up, and if Joey and Ruby were standing up, there had to be loads more like them who were either working behind the scenes or wanting to. A lot of people were probably unsure of how to help.

When the idea occurred to me, I was ashamed of myself for not thinking of it sooner. "Social media," I whispered.

"What's that, love?" Ruby looked up from her book.

"I know what we have to do next before we attempt a hit on the prison. We need to spread the word about ourselves, make people see that we're not to be feared, that we're the victims. People across the nation, across the world, need to see for themselves that they're not alone, that there are women like us out there who are fighting, who are resisting. That we aren't hurting people, we're defending ourselves, that we only want to live our lives."

Joey stood with his keys dangling from his fingers. "Do you think it will work? We'll have to upload anonymously, from somewhere public. We can't upload from the bar."

"What can it hurt? If anything, we can give people something to hold on to, something to hope for, without giving them specifics of our plans." I hopped off the barstool, teetering a little. "I need to close my eyes before I fall over. Joey, go grab some food and while you're out, look around for somewhere close by where we can upload a video."

Joey nodded, tossing up his keys and catching them again. "You got it."

The cot was cozier than I was expecting. I thought sleep would be impossible, that with everything spinning around in my mind, I'd never find it. I was wrong.

****

When I woke, I felt a warm body pressed up against my back. I turned my head and saw a flash of blonde hair. Billie was in a deep sleep, her mouth gaping open as she breathed rhythmically.

I didn't want to disturb her but needed the bathroom, not to mention my back was stiff. The cot wasn't exactly comfortable for long sleep. It was essentially a metal frame with the world's thinnest mattress laid over the top. My face was nearly pressed to the wall, so I used the concrete wall to balance myself as I slid away from Billie. Managing to get to my knees, I scooted down the length of the cot until I was free. I hadn't woken her. She continued breathing heavily in a way I'd never heard from her.

The suitcase given to me by Ruby sat under a desk, the chipped wooden top littered with all manner of papers and receipts. Joey must have been as good at keeping records as I was.

I pulled out the suitcase, kneeling down to snap it open and pull out fresh clothes. Finding something that smelled fresh was the trick. I grabbed a white tank top and my plaid skirt, along with some clean underwear. A skirt was not the most practical item of clothing when fighting for your life, but it would do for now until we were ready for the next mission.

The bathroom was not as clean as Joey had made out. Whereas the sheets had smelled freshly washed, the bathroom was as dingy as the one in the bar, with a mildewy smell that make me think of mold. Joey was a bachelor, so I tried not to judge him too harshly as I wrinkled up my nose.

I had my own bar of soap, taken from the bathroom at the school, along with a small bottle of lotion, shampoo, and conditioner. I'd managed to hang on to a small bag of makeup that I'd yet to use but figured if we were going to film a video then today was the day.

As I showered, the water, as hot as I could get it, scouring away all the film from the last two days, I thought about the content for the video. People wouldn't want to see filthy women, tired and sickly, even if it was more real to show people that we'd been through hell.

The public would want to see clean, put together women, strong and determined to do the right thing. That was the way of the media in all its glory.

We'd make ourselves look as presentable as possible, blink away the exhaustion to appear tough, and we'd stand under the sun and declare that we were afraid but not backing down. We were standing up. We were fighting the madness, defending ourselves and others, and that other women who felt able should do the same.

That was when another thought struck me. How were these women supposed to stand up for themselves when they hadn't the slightest idea of how to control their powers? They'd have to be taught. The single most important lesson in the grimoire was about finding your touchstone and focusing your power. So, why not give women around the globe a crash course? Maybe we'd make two videos. In case one was taken down, there would be more of a chance of word getting out.

This wouldn't take long. The hardest part would be getting to a café where we could use their Wi-Fi to upload.

I stepped out of the shower to towel off.

If we were going to hit the old prison and attempt to get our people out, these videos would be a life insurance policy. Because if we didn't make it out, if we were taken or worse, we'd need other women out there, women like us, who could change the world.

When I emerged back into the office, Billie was gone. Aromas of the most delicious kind wafted through the open door. I followed the scent back into the bar.

Neeta brushed by me, her mouth half full. "Joey did good with the food, and he told me about your video idea. Which I like, by the way. Off to the shower."

I didn't have to be told about the food twice. As I rounded the corner, I spied open containers all along the bar top. Billie, Joey, and Ruby sat in the banquette.

Joey pointed to the bar. "Grab a paper plate and load up, Miranda."

I did as I was told. There were BBQ ribs, pulled pork, baked beans, corn on the cob, biscuits, coleslaw, and cold cans of orange soda. I helped myself to heaping portions of everything, sitting on a bar stool at the end of the bar, only feet away from the others.

The food smelled like heaven. I ate three huge bites before I was able to speak. "I was thinking about the video in the shower. I think we should make two, if time allows. We'll give the lesson from the grimoire, the one about control, and we'll talk about what we're doing, without giving specifics. I want other women out there to know they're capable, you know? That they don't have to roll over and accept this."

"I like it." Billie sat in front of her empty plate of food. She looked rested and happy. She'd broken out her blue babydoll dress. It was my absolute favorite thing she'd ever worn. She also wore her black Doc Martens, which I didn't think she'd taken with us. At least, I didn't think she had.

"Billie, where did the boots come from? I thought you left those behind."

"I did." She jabbed a thumb in Joeys' direction. "Tell her," she said to him.

"I almost forgot." Joey inclined his head to the pool table behind me. "Trapper cleaned out the rest of your things, all three of you. He wanted you to have your stuff but didn't know where to take it or send it, so he took it all to Ruby's."

Ruby smiled. "I went to the club while you were sleeping to pick your things up. Thought you might want some of it."

I swiveled in the seat to see the suitcase I'd left

behind along with my guitar, sitting on the green felt.

There were no words. I slid off the stool and dashed to the suitcase, throwing it open to reveal all the vintage beauties I'd left in the closet at the Fleur de Lis. My beautiful black dresses, the ones I'd worn on stage at Ruby's, were folded neatly inside. Along with some other clothing I hadn't been able to fit, and which I'd deemed impractical such as my favorite sundress and a pair of velvet bell bottoms. The gloves I bought from the vintage store on Magazine Street the first day I'd hung out with Billie were there, as well as the bracelet, my other jewelry, and my bottle of Chanel Number 5.

I ran my fingers over everything. "How sweet of Trapper to do this for us." My voice broke, and I had to force back tears lest I ruin the first makeup I'd worn in a week. Crying over material things was probably ridiculous, anyway. Still, I was grateful to have it all back.

"Grumpy old man isn't quite as grumpy as he makes out. He packed up all the stuff I left behind too. Even my bedding and my little pink TV. That stuff is all still at Ruby's. He packed up all Neeta's stuff too."

"Can you believe I left my favorite pair of dress shorts and my favorite Hawaiian shirt?" Neeta emerged from the back, fresh from her shower wearing exactly the clothing she'd described. Her navy pin-striped shorts were the perfect complement to the sailor blue shirt emblazoned with bright pink hibiscus flowers.

"I guess we all felt like dressing up today." I smiled at Neeta, who was glowing for the first time since we left New Orleans.

She returned my smile. "There's something hopeful in what we're doing. Spreading a message of love to others like us. What better reason to dress up?"

"Exactly," Billie said, sliding out of the banquette

to join us. "Then, we'll go kick some ass and free the rest of our family."

The three of us stood in a circle in the middle of the Trumpet, holding hands like we were about to cast a spell. Instead, we just held on to each other, reveling in the moment, the moment before everything would change.

****

Since the Trumpet was our only real safe haven, we decided to find somewhere neutral to film, somewhere that were the background identified, it wouldn't cause us any harm.

"This cannot be filmed outdoors." Neeta was walking in a circle around the pool table, her hands shoved in the pockets of her shorts. "All it takes is one spy and we're toast. But we can't film anywhere that could be identified and could get anyone in trouble."

"What about the little stone building Miranda found outside of New Orleans?" Billie sat at the bar, her long legs swinging underneath her.

I shook my head, my legs tucked up underneath as I sat on the pool table. "Henry knows about it, remember? There's a possibility it's being watched."

"I looked at a couple of empty buildings lately. I was contemplating moving Ruby's into a bigger space, before the world seemed to go into hiding. How about a break-in?" Ruby sat at the bar next to Billie.

Joey, behind the bar, his arms crossed as he leaned against the cash register, frowned. "I don't know about that. There are sure to be cameras, alarm systems. If we trip something, there won't be enough time to film."

"Couldn't we disrupt the cameras? With our energy? Flickering lights and all." Billie had a point. Before we'd known more about our energy, lights flickering around us was a common experience.

Neeta stopped walking in a circle, her hand resting on the green velvet of the pool table. "Genius thought, Bill. With that in mind, I think I know the perfect place. It isn't glamorous, by any means, but it'll get the job done, and there's never anyone there."

"Where?" I asked, unease moving through me. I didn't want to take too long to get this video made. My hope was that we'd be in Shreveport, hitting the prison before dawn.

"My dad had a storage unit in mid-city. Whenever I went with him the place was always deserted. We hop the fence, go in the back, break into a unit, and film."

"Won't they be full of stuff?"

Neeta shrugged. "There's sure to be a lot of empty units. As I said, the place was always deserted."

"I don't know." My knees bounced. "I'm getting antsy. We want to head to Shreveport tonight, right? It's a five-hour drive. We need to go to this place, break in, disable cameras, find an empty unit, film, and then upload the video. All before we can leave town. Maybe the video was a bad idea. We're running out of time."

"Which is exactly why we need the video." Ruby crossed one long leg over the other. "Take whatever you'll need to go to Shreveport with you to this storage facility. I'll follow. You film the video on my phone. You guys split from there, and I'll handle the upload. Then I'll smash my phone and head back here. I won't go back to Ruby's or my house."

"Ruby..." Neeta shook her head from side to side. "Absolutely not. If you do that, you could end up a fugitive like us."

"Well, I guess this will just have to work, won't it? We won't get anywhere if we don't make a ruckus. What's that line about well-behaving women never making history?"

Billie laid her head on Ruby's shoulder. Ruby patted her thigh.

"All right." Joey looked tired. He rubbed his eyes. "You three get ready. I know you all wanted to be cute for the video, but practical is best if we're going straight to Shreveport. I'll drive us all in my truck. Ruby will follow. Then, we'll take the truck to Shreveport."

"We'll need another vehicle. What if there are more women than we can cram in the bed of the truck? The gray suit dick said there were twenty something, right? A van or bus would be ideal." I didn't know where we were going to get a bus, but if we were at the point of breaking into storage facilities and prisons, why not add car theft to the rap sheet.

Neeta dug her hand in a pocket of the pool table, clacking balls together. "Our best bet will be at the prison. They'll have vehicles like that there. It won't be any harder to take a bus than it will be to release all the women. We've had no time to plan, to look at the prison's layout. Winging it is our only option. Has been our only option from the beginning."

"Neeta's right." Joey leaned forward, his hands on the bar behind Billie. "Step one is getting there, step two is getting in, step three is going to be whatever it is, subduing guards, freeing women—whatever is thrown at you. Escape won't be until step four or five. I'm nervous." He hung his head.

Billie turned around, reaching out both hands to her love. "We'll be okay. Just keep the truck running. We'll be out in no time."

The confidence in her voice in no way matched the wariness I felt inside. I was sure Billie and Neeta both felt that wariness too. There was no way they couldn't.

I looked around the bar that was the Trumpet and

thought back to my first night there. It was the night we'd walked on Bourbon Street and Billie had pointed out the bare-chested ladies flashing their breasts at people for beads. How shocked I'd been. I remembered how we'd walked here, a quieter part of the Quarter that I loved. The buildings were old, the gas-lit lamps casting an eerie, beautiful glow over rough stone. The inside of the bar was where Billie had flirted with Joey while Neeta drank her red-colored cocktails, laughing with me over joke after joke. I had been so scared, but the world had seemed fuller of possibility. Now the world just seemed bleak. There was no guarantee we would be successful, no guarantee we would free anyone, no guarantee we would even find our loved ones. But we had to try. Ruby was right about one thing, we had to be loud; we had to cause a ruckus. Sitting down, hiding in the darkness, not wanting to cause trouble, was a path that led to even more suppression.

So, we dressed. Even though it was the middle of the day and a thousand degrees, there was no choice but to dress in jeans, comfortable shoes, and the darkest tops we could find. For me that was a black turtleneck, tightly fitted but stretchy. Billie wore a long sleeve black hoodie, and Neeta wore a black polo shirt. She literally had nothing with long sleeves, except a hoodie she hated.

By the time we made it to the storage facility, late afternoon was sliding into evening. Antsy couldn't even begin to describe how I felt. My body shook with nerves, anxiety churned in my stomach. Focusing on anything other than Ash and the hell she had gone through, all because of me, was all I could do. Filming the video, driving the five hours to Shreveport, I wasn't sure how I would bear it. I just wanted to get there.

Joey pulled his giant truck through an alley. There was a closed and abandoned grocery store on one side, the chain link fence that served as security for the storage unit on the other.

The fence was about eight feet high, but other than the height, would not be too difficult to climb.

"From what I remember," Neeta said, "the only cameras are on the front of the units, so we should be safe for several feet once we get over the fence."

I bounced on the backseat, my gaze trained on the long rows of metal boxes, gray and indistinct in every way.

"The place looks as derelict as the grocery store over there. I'm pretty sure this place is out of business." Billie gazed in the same direction as everyone else.

Neeta leaned farther over my shoulder to peer out the glass. "You might be right. Maybe something will finally go our way."

Billie swung her head around, snapping Neeta with a ferocious look. "Don't jinx us."

"Okay, forget I said it. Let's just go." Neeta nudged my leg, which I guessed meant to open the door.

Ruby pulled behind us, her tires crunching gravel. We all glanced at her through the rear window. She turned off her car, giving us one solemn nod. Neeta already held Ruby's phone in her hand. The three of us would scale the fence, make the video, then head back where we would hand off the phone to Ruby. She would take off to upload our video for the world, and Joey would drive us the long way to Shreveport.

With a quick kiss for Joey, Billie was the first to open her door.

I followed suit, Neeta sliding out behind me.

She tucked the phone in her back pocket before taking to the fence.

I couldn't remember the last time I'd climbed a fence, sometime during childhood surely, but I didn't remember it being so hard. Maybe it was knowing that Joey and Ruby intently watched our progress, or maybe it was my own lack of athleticism, but I struggled with every foot and hand hold. Neeta and Billie seemed to zoom right to the top, and they were both older than me by a few years. That humiliating thought made me try to climb faster, which only succeeded in almost causing me to fall twice.

In the end, I made it over.

The three of us stood on the other side of the fence.

Billie dropped into a crouch which made Neeta laugh. "I don't think anyone is here," she said between snorts.

Billie stood up, holding her head high. "You never know."

There was an eerie silence as if the business had, indeed, gone belly up. All I could hear was the sound of distant traffic.

"Let's go straight to the first locker. There's no way to know if the cameras are still on, so let's disable the ones in our immediate vicinity to be safe." Neeta led the way. We crept between two of the long storage buildings. Neeta stopped at the corner, peering around the side. The sharp smell of metal siding baking in the sun permeated the air. "There are four cameras that will be able to see us. Miranda, you take out the one across the way. Billie, you take the one to the right, and I'll manage the two aimed at this unit." She patted the wall. "Ready?"

"Go," I said, moving around Neeta. I let the magic build in my palm, the blue light dancing, careful to control the blast. I didn't want to alert the whole block to our presence. I raised my hand, shooting one quick blast at the camera hanging under the eave of the opposite storage building. The shot hit the camera dead on. The reverberation was loud, but not loud enough that I thought it could be heard very far.

Billie did the same, shooting the camera to our right. Neeta handled her two cameras in the same way.

Billie bounced up and down. "You guys," she squealed. "Can you believe how good we're getting at this? Before we would have taken down half the buildings in a shower of rubble."

Neeta suppressed a smile. "Yay, we're getting so good at wielding our magic powers." The sarcasm was thick in her voice.

"Whatever, I think it's cool." Billie pointed to the storage unit. "No lock."

"Thank the goddess, the less noise we have to make, the better." Neeta popped the handle open.

I leaned into the heavy metal, garage-like door, helping her to push it up.

"Ew." I stepped back with a cough. The inside of the unit, large and empty, smelled absolutely rancid. "I can't go in there. Let's pick another one."

Neeta wrinkled up her nose. "They'll all smell the same. That's moisture, rot, and mold. The best we can do is let it air out for a minute, then film this video in one go. The mold won't kill us in twenty minutes."

"Let's run through the script one more time, then." Billie stood the farthest from the opening.

"Right." I planted my feet, concentrating on what we'd already discussed. "Billie films, Neeta gives the control lesson, I give the pep talk, then we cut. Pretty simple."

"Simple is always best. Especially since we don't know how long the video will be out there before it's taken down." She slipped the phone from her pocket, handing it to Billie.

"Just one video then? I thought we were filming

two." Billie swiped her finger around the screen as she talked.

I bounced from foot to foot. All I wanted to do was get on our way. The better idea would be to wait a few, let the day slip away a little more so that we were arriving in the middle of the night, but I was anxious, a knot the size of Pittsburgh in my stomach eating its way through the lining of my gut. "One video is enough. I know it was my idea to film two, but Neeta's right."

Neeta's nerves were getting the better of her too. I could tell. She was pinching the skin on the side of her arm, something I noticed she was doing more and more. She did this whenever we were in a tough spot. She nodded. "Yeah, we need to get a move on." She turned on her heel, walking farther into the musty stink of the storage unit.

The air inside was cool. This was one welcome relief.

I stood to the side as Neeta took center stage. Billie stopped about ten feet away from her, holding up the phone. "Just tell me when you're ready."

There was plenty of light from the bright sun outside. This flooded the space in a rather dramatic fashion which I found fitting.

Neeta cracked her knuckles. "Go."

Billie tapped the screen, then pointed a finger at Neeta.

We'd agreed there would be no introductions, no long-winded speech before the lesson. The lesson was the most important thing, the speech secondary.

"Control," Neeta began. "Is attained more easily than you might think. At first, your insides feel chaotic, but all you have to do is slow down, find your breath, find your center." Neeta pulled her red sandstone from her pocket. "Find an element from nature, something you can tether yourself to, like a touchstone. This will be different for everyone. Go outside, walk around, focus on finding your object, and it will come to you. This object can be anything natural, anything small enough to fit in your hand. A rock, a gem, a piece of wood, an acorn. You'll know your object when you find it." Neeta was talking faster than normal, but still slow enough as to be understood.

"Once you have your touchstone, hold it in one hand. With your other hand, reach out with your palm up and breathe. Don't suppress your emotions. Let whatever is happening in your life wash over you. Let it all flow. Concentrate on feeling your power in the palm of your hand. Hold it there. When you feel ready, push it from you, then reel it back in. You will not master this on the first try. Keep going. When you feel ready to move on, push the energy out farther, then out farther, reeling it back each time. Again, when you feel ready, release your energy as a pulse toward an object—you can control how much power you send out at any given time. Practice sending out just a stunning pulse, then a larger one. Master each step before moving to the next. Once you get going, once you become more and more confident, this will become easier. Good luck."

Neeta stepped aside so quickly that I was momentarily stunned, not quite ready for the spotlight. This was a far different spotlight than the one I was used to. This was not me singing other people's songs. This was me giving a rousing pep talk. I hadn't even prepared anything to say, which I now realized was stupid.

I stumbled to the center of the storage unit. I cleared my throat. I swallowed.

Billie made the universal sign for *hurry up.*

I took a deep breath. "Hi," I said, stupidly. "The world is a terrifying place for anyone with a womb or anyone who finds themselves outside the norm. We know. We know what you're going through. I've had to run from my home. I've lost my family, and so have my friends. But it doesn't have to be scary, or at least, it can be less scary. I know that if I were having to do this alone, I probably wouldn't have made it so far. We have become each other's family, and we have others who aren't like us but who are allies, people who are in our corner, who've put themselves in danger. So, what I'm saying is this—find your people. They may be other" —I hesitated— "witches, or they may be boyfriends or parents, or teachers, or neighbors. Your people are out there. Find each other. Practice control. That lesson is everything at the beginning, and there are more, more lessons that we hope to share as time goes on. We can fight them. We don't have to hurt anyone or kill anyone, but we can and should protect ourselves. What's happening to us is wrong. If we all stand up together, shoulder to shoulder, with other witches and with our allies, the government, the authorities, *they,* whatever you call them, they have to stop, they have to listen. They won't have a choice. We have a voice, and we will all use it. Help each other. Give each other shelter. Teach those who don't get to see this video, spread the knowledge, spread the love. Good luck to us all."

Billie tapped the screen, a tear streaking down her cheek. "That was good." Her voice cracked.

"It was good," Neeta said. "Now let's hand this off to Ruby and get out of New Orleans."

I took a step back. I'd spoken so quickly and for so long, I had almost no breath. All I could do was nod as I followed them into the blinding light of mid-day.

We jogged back to the gate, once again scaling the fence and landing back on the other side. Billie ran the phone to Ruby, plopping the phone in her waiting hand, held out the window. Ruby pulled Billie down close, said something to her, nodded once to us, then reversed out of the alley and off to do her part.

Neeta and I slipped back into Joey's air-conditioned truck, the engine running.

Billie got in, slamming the door behind her and sinking down into the plush seat.

"What did Ruby say?" I asked as I buckled in for the long ride.

"She said, don't die. Tell Neeta and Miranda not to die either."

Chapter Sixteen

After having driven to Colorado and back, I would have thought the drive to Shreveport would be easy. It wasn't. The drive felt like the longest I'd ever been on. It was five hours of pure torture. Not only was I so sick and tired of being in a car I could scream, but I was also more on edge than I'd been in my life. Billie had laid her head on Joey's lap while he drove, and she was currently snoring softly from the front seat.

Neeta sat slumped next to me, her head lolling around her shoulders, but I knew she wasn't asleep, only trying to rest. Every now and then she opened her eyes, lifted her head, and scanned the surrounding scenery, then folded back into her uncomfortable looking position.

I couldn't even try to close my eyes, although they drooped with exhaustion. My eyelids were heavy, my limbs were heavy, my heart was heavy. All I wanted to do was speed up time. Oh, how I wished that was a power I had. Maybe I did and one day I would learn it, but today was not that day. All I could do in the meantime was bounce from one butt cheek to the other, cross and uncross my legs, chew my nails, and bang my head repeatedly against the headrest.

I watched the minutes tick by on the truck's clock. When four and a half hours had gone by, feeling more like ten, Joey pulled off onto a dirt road. As soon as the truck stopped, Neeta's head jerked up. "Are we here?"

"Almost," he said. "We're a half hour out. I thought we should have a restroom break and that maybe you three should discuss your plan a bit more. I'm a little nervous about your plan as I keep saying."

"You mean lack of one?" I said through a yawn. "A bathroom break and regroup is a great idea."

"Billie." Joey shook Billie. It took him about four tries to wake the girl. I swear she could sleep like the dead.

We all exited the truck, Joey going off in one direction to relieve himself while the three of us went in another.

"We don't want to go too far off the road," Neeta said as she led us.

Once we had finished our business and were standing in the truck lights, stretching our backs and legs, Billie began. "So, we know there's an access road about a mile from the jail. That's going to be the closest we can get for a sneak attack."

This had been an ongoing debate. Did we sneak up on the prison or did we blow through the gates and go in hands a blazing? I was for the latter.

"If we park that far away, how will we get everyone out? They'll be drugged."

"We think they'll be drugged." Neeta rolled her head in a circle. "The point is we don't know what to expect so should plan for all outcomes. I think Joey should drop us off at the access road. We'll sneak through the fence, across the grounds, then inside. It's best if we keep them in the dark for as long as possible. Two of us finds the women, while one of us finds a vehicle. Whoever goes for the vehicle keeps an ear out. It probably won't be too hard to find each other once the fighting starts. If we need more transportation that's when one of us can get Joey. Otherwise, he stays put until we can tell him we're on the way out. Let's not make this more complicated than it needs to be. How does that sound?"

Neeta was forever the practical one. I hated to admit she was right, that we had to keep our heads and keep our cover as long as possible.

"Fine," I said.

Billie nodded. "Who's doing what?"

"Miranda and I go inside to find the women. You find transport."

Billie's mouth scrunched up. She flicked a glance over at Joey who leaned against the front bumper of his truck. "I don't like the idea of splitting up. We've made it this far because we've stayed together."

"We absolutely have," Neeta said. "But this is not our usual circumstance. The stakes have never been higher. We have to divide and conquer."

Billie nodded, her gaze dropping to the ground.

I understood how Billie felt, because I felt the same way. If this went wrong, if one of us fell, which was a very real possibility, I wanted us to be together. What if Billie fell all alone, or what if Neeta or I did, and Billie wasn't able to say goodbye? Splitting up seemed the worst possible thing we could do, but Neeta was right, it had to be done. There was too much to do and too little time in which to do it.

Neeta took Billie's hand, and then mine. I reached for Billie's. We were three little witches whose mettle was about to be tested to no end. I only hoped we would succeed. The most important thing was that the world see that we were not going to take being jailed and held against our will. We were going to stand up and fight the injustice of it. All it would take was one act of bravery to light the whole world on fire. We were about to light that fire, consequences be damned.

"You three ready?" Joey hadn't said anything until then. He knew this was our fight, as difficult as it probably was for him to watch Billie run off into battle without him.

I looked him right in the eye. "As ready as we're going to be."

Night had fully fallen a couple of hours prior to our arrival. Joey turned off his lights, doing his best to navigate the back woods road with only the light from the stars as our guide. The moon was only a sliver, and I was glad for this. The darker the night, the better.

"I hope I don't pop a tire in one of these deep ruts." Joey leaned forward over his steering wheel, navigating the darkness as best as he could.

The rest of us bounced along, silent. I could only assume Neeta and Billie were as terrified as I was. I tried not to think too far ahead. it was best to focus on one step at a time—park the car, find our way to the prison yard fence, clip our way through with the wire cutters Joey thought to pack into a toolbox, cross the yard, break off with Billie as she went her way and we went ours, find the others, find Ash and Crystal, and then get the hell out.

If I started thinking too far ahead, those images in my mind quickly became distorted by my fear. I saw Indiana Jones-like melting faces, buildings blown to rubble, bodies at my feet.

We came to a jerking stop. Joey pointed out the window. "There's the fence." He said this quietly, in almost a whisper like there were people lurking who could hear us speaking inside the truck. He dropped his pointing finger to Billie's arm.

Neeta tugged my shirt sleeve. "Let's slide out and give them a moment." She opened her door, took a look around, then dropped to the ground.

I followed.

We stood in the dead quiet, crickets chirping in the night. Even those seemed so far away.

Neeta gripped the wire cutters in one hand, letting the heavy tool dangle next to her leg. "Are you ready for this?" she asked. "We're not playing around anymore.

Some real, heavy shit is about to go down."

I wanted to point out that I hadn't felt we'd been playing in a long time. Some serious shit had gone down the second I landed in New Orleans, but I also understood her meaning. The fake holding facility had been playtime compared to this. We were in real danger. All of us were. Letting Billie go off by herself seemed the worst possible idea, but what choice did we have? Finding a way out was vital. The best way to do that while also finding our people was to split up. The one thing you should never do in any horror movie.

When Billie got out of the car, she looked away, off into the inky forest.

Neeta reached out her free hand, stroking Billie's arm, only once. Then she stalked off toward the fence, Billie and I scrambling after her. This was it—the time had come to test our resolve against an enemy we knew little about.

At the fence line, Neeta dropped to her knees in the dirt. She began clipping at fencing. I held back wires as she continued to cut a body sized hole. She dropped the wire cutter, then crawled through.

Billie went next.

When it was my turn, they held it for me.

I half expected some sort of alarm to sound the second we were inside the perimeter, but nothing happened.

"Let's go. I want to get this the hell over with." Billie took off in a crouch-walk, her head swiveling from side to side.

Neeta and I followed.

The back part of the property was mostly grass, tall and unmowed. Walking through it gave me the creeps. I tried thinking of anything other than ticks and spiders.

We stopped behind a shed about twenty yards from the rear of the prison. The large, rectangular, brick building was lit up like a Christmas tree, light pouring from every window. Floodlights filled the yard between where we hid behind the shed and the back wall of the prison. Men and women with guns on their hips and terrifying shotguns in their hands stood at posts between us and our target, the back entrance. I couldn't see them but had to assume that snipers would be positioned above us as well.

"There won't be any way to sneak by them," I said, my voice barely above a whisper.

"One of us will have to create a distraction." Billie crouched by my side, her gaze on the side of the building where several large buses stood at the ready.

"Absolutely not," I breathed in her ear.

"Look." Billie spun on the balls of her feet. "We knew what we were getting into here, but I think we can distract the guards in the opposite direction, then circumvent the madness. I can break off to sneak inside one of those buses, while the two of you head in the back door."

"They won't all break off, some of them will stay put." Neeta's brow pinched, and her eyes looked pained.

"Then we deal with those the best we can. We can do this, you guys. We have to."

I inhaled a deep breath. Billie was right. We'd come this far. There was nothing left to do but keep going.

She didn't wait for us to come to a verbal agreement. With one quick nod, Billie spun back around, raised her hand, and shot a fearsome blast at a set of workout equipment sitting at the far side of the yard.

Immediately, all eyes and pointed guns were raised in that direction. Half of the guards broke off, while the other half stayed put.

Neeta and I responded without hesitation. Palms out, we rushed the remaining guards, Billie sneaking off behind us to find a bus. It was imperative we keep her undercover, the focus on us and us alone.

We managed to shock-blast three guards each before the bullets began flying. By then, we were halfway to the door. I couldn't turn around to see what had become of Billie. All I could do was continue running and shooting energy from my hands. I no longer needed my touchstone. I just needed to know that my life and the lives of my family depended on reaching that door and gaining access to the jail.

Three more successful shots and we were almost there—mere steps away.

Then, all was pain. All was searing, unimaginable pain. I went down on one knee, my left hand clutching my side. Bullets and bolts of energy continued to whiz past.

"Get up," Neeta screamed.

I heard metal give way right before Neeta gripped my upper arm, hauling me to my feet and into a cold, brightly lit hallway. A door slammed behind us. I slumped against the far wall. Through the fog that was my mind, I saw Neeta take her hand and smear it down the side of the door where it met the frame, fusing the metal together with the energy from her hand.

"How did you know you could do that?" I breathed through the pain in my side.

"I didn't, but lucky for us." She stooped next to me. "Miranda we can't stop here. How bad is it." She pulled my hand from my side. Blood poured from the wound. "Fuck."

I sucked in a breath as she pulled me up and then turned me around. "It looks like the bullet went straight through your side. God, it's bleeding a lot."

"Seal it," I said, my body beginning to feel light, my head fuzzy.

"What?"

"Seal it like you did the door."

"Miranda, you're not a door and I'm not a doctor."

I teetered to the side, Neeta catching me by my elbow. "Do it, Neeta. We read about this in the grimoire. If I lose any more blood, I'm not going to make it. I certainly won't be any more use to you."

"Fuck," Neeta said again. She lifted my shirt. "Deep breath."

A hot, burning pain seared my flesh. I heard the sizzle, smelled the meat cooking. I almost wretched, almost screamed, but instead, I choked on a sob. I bit into my tongue until I tasted blood.

"I'm sorry. One more time." Neeta laid her palm on the exit wound, the same searing pain wracking my senses. I fell into her. Neeta wrapped her arms around my waist. "Can you continue?"

I breathed through the nausea, my body shuddering. Sweat poured down my face, obscuring my vision. The pain had done one thing at least—it had woken me back up. I nodded against her shoulder.

Yelling and footsteps echoed off down the long corridor. "Time to go." Neeta pushed me back, taking my hand and pulling me after her down the hallway in the opposite direction.

We turned, heading farther inside the labyrinth of the jail. The floors were old linoleum, scuffed and yellowed, the walls cold concrete devoid of any color or ornamentation. This was a place you could get lost in forever.

As I ran, I began to feel, not exactly better, but

less like I was going to die. Fresh adrenaline coursed through my body. I pulled my hand from Neeta's, doing everything in my power to concentrate, to listen.

"Hold on. Stop." I pulled at the back of Neeta's shirt. "I hear something."

"Me, too. Guards yelling and chasing after us."

"No, I hear crying."

Neeta's eyes went wide. "I hear it too. Up ahead." She turned and took off down the corridor. At the end, we stopped to listen again.

"That way," I said, pushing Neeta on.

"Why is there no one around?" Neeta whispered. "Something's wrong."

"All we can do is keep going." I pulled her to a stop. "The crying is coming from in there."

We'd entered a cluster of offices, something that reminded me a lot of the offices at my high school. This area was carpeted with a cheap, rust colored carpet, and there was a musty smell like old stale cigarettes and a decades old coffeepot that hadn't been cleaned in eons.

Through a window, I spied a slight girl with a cloud of pink hair sitting on a flea-bitten couch, her head in her hands.

"Oh my god, it's Lou." I pointed past Neeta, who took off at a sprint to the closed office door.

Chapter Seventeen

The door opened.

Lou raised her head, eyes red and bloodshot. "What?" she asked, then recognition dawned. "Did they get you too?"

I shook my head. "No, we're breaking you and the others out. Come on."

She didn't budge from her seat, just continued looking back and forth between Neeta and me, her blood red eyes bulging from her small face. "You haven't been taken into custody?" She smiled through her tears, then finally stood up. "Do you have the grimoire? The rest of it?" Her voice raised an octave as if she were excited.

"That hardly matters now. Come on. We need to get to the others. Do you know where they are?" I pulled on her arm, hoping to get her to wipe that weird expression off her face and tell us where our people were. We did have the grimoire. The pages were jammed in Joey's glove box. Now I was beginning to wonder if that was such a good idea.

"Of course I know where the others are, but the most important thing is that I know where the grimoire is. Do you have it on you or not?"

Neeta shot me a glance with a warning behind it. Something was off here.

"Why are you in here alone? And why haven't you been put in a cell and drugged with the others?" I backed away from the girl, wiping the sweat from my hands on the back of my jeans.

Neeta raised her arm by a degree but didn't extend it all the way.

That's when I noticed the phone sitting on the couch where she'd been. Someone was on the other end, listening to our conversation.

"What did you do?" I asked, disbelief coursing through me.

"What I had to. For my dad, and for my country."

Neeta raised her hand, but it was too late. The main area of the office was flooded with guards. Out the window, I could see one of the gray-suited men, the one we'd controlled at the school. I could also see the resemblance. How did I not notice before? They both had small eyes, thin lips, and rotten smiles.

"Your dad, right."

We were stuck, trapped in the small office with Lou, the traitor, while outside we were surrounded.

She approached me. "I suspected you had it after we tried sneaking out. Then I realized getting it from you would be easier than getting it from Bea. Even under my spell, she was stubborn about the grimoire, and as many times as I searched her room, I couldn't find that stupid book. You're the one who always seemed in charge of the pages. I guess since it was your stupid aunt who wrote the thing, I'm going to guess the book is on you." She put her hands on me then, groping through the pockets of my jeans. A hand grazed my wound.

I sucked in a breath through gritted teeth, stopping myself just in time before I slapped her back. "You put a spell on my aunt? That's what was wrong with her." *What an idiot.* I should have known all along that what changed Aunt Bea wasn't natural. My chest constricted as I saw her lying on the floor in the foyer, a huge bump on her head. We'd attacked each other because of this bitch.

Lou's tiny hand dipped into the back pocket of my jeans, the pocket where, until recently, I'd kept my portion of the grimoire's pages. She withdrew her hands from my body. I'd never felt so violated, so disgusted by another human being, and I'd been in the presence of Dave, Billie's old john.

"You, then." Lou stepped up to Neeta, groping her in the same manner she'd groped me. When she came up empty for the second time, the triumphant look that had been plastered on her face fell. Her gaze dropped to the carpet for a split second before shooting a glance at her dad who stood so still he looked like a wax statue. "The other one must have it."

Lou looked back at Neeta, then at me. "Where is Billie anyway?"

"She couldn't make it." Neeta sneered at her, her upper lip baring teeth.

"Too bad for the three of you. With the book you at least had some value. Now you have none." Lou folded her arms across her chest.

"Not so hasty, Louise." Robo-dad broke off from the guards flanking him to step into our small room. "Clearly, they've stashed the book somewhere. Somewhere nearby, no doubt. You'll learn more about interrogation with experience."

Lou's face went red, and I wondered how badly she wanted his approval. She'd gone to such lengths to get it only to have him publicly dismiss her. I would have gloated had we not been in such trouble. As it was, I gave her a smug smile.

He gestured to the twenty or so guards behind him. "Take these two to holding cell 9. Don't drug them quite yet. I have questions."

I tried not to look at Neeta but hoped she was thinking the same thing I was. Without the drugs in our system, we'd still be able to fight. There was also the chance that if they were taking us to a holding cell, we'd be closer to our targets. Maybe getting caught hadn't been such bad luck after all.

My only worries at this point were two-fold—what had happened to Billie, and would Joey be able to stay off their radar? Billie had eluded them thus far. If they'd had her, they would have said, but where was she? It seemed too much to hope for that she'd made it to one of the buses, and if she had, it would be an absolute miracle had she managed to sneak inside one.

But I was thinking too far ahead again.

Stay focused, Miranda. One step at a time.

The next step was allowing the guards—there seemed so many around us—to usher us to holding cell 9. One giant man, stubble all across his face and neck, pulled my hands roughly behind my back, securing them with a zip tie. Another man, not nearly the size of mine, was spinning Neeta around to do the same. He then pushed her forward, the giant pushing me along to follow.

We were prodded back down the long, cold corridor, back the way we had come. When we passed the back doors, the doors we'd come through, which were still sealed by Neeta's magic, I knew that being caught had been the luckiest thing to happen to us. We'd been going in the wrong direction.

The guards wound us through corridor after corridor until we reached our first security checkpoint. At least that's what I assumed it to be. We were buzzed through a door, probably bulletproof, then immediately buzzed through another door. We were now in the jail proper.

The catwalk we walked on looked down over a space I assumed was some sort of general population mixing area with metal picnic style tables and benches. Flanking this area on all sides were cells. The more I peered into these cells, all below us, as we walked by, my eyes adjusting to the dim lighting, the more came into focus. I tried not to gasp at the sight. Slumbering bodies appeared to inhabit the bed of every cell we passed. So far, I'd counted fourteen people. From where we were on the catwalk it was impossible to tell if any of these women were Ash or Crystal, but they were there. I knew they were.

The air was frigid cold, so cold I could see my breath. The temperature must have something to do with keeping the women in these slumbering states. Drugs and cold, drugs and cold.

Neeta, ahead of me, the smaller guard gripping her upper arm like a vise, was shoved into an open cell. I was shocked they'd been instructed to keep us together. Putting us together seemed an error of judgment.

The cell door banged shut behind us. Then all was silence. There were two bunk beds in this cell, a toilet, and a sink, both streaked with rust and grime.

The guards who had manhandled us all the way here stood sentry outside, their backs to us. I could see no other guards. Once we'd gone through the security doors, we'd left the entourage behind.

I glanced at Neeta, who gave me one solemn nod. Her bicep tensed. I immediately knew what she was doing. There was no other way to get out of our bonds. Warmth suffused my palm as I twisted my wrist as far as it would go. Melting the plastic of the zip tie was the only way to get it off without alerting the guards that something was up. The edge of my palm touched plastic. I had to hope that I was close enough to melt the tie.

I breathed through the surge of energy, allowing only enough to heat without sending a blast through the back wall of the cell. There was a pull in the plastic. It was working. I focused. The plastic became hot, gooping onto the tender flesh inside my wrist. I bit down on my lip to keep from whimpering. The plastic burned and the heat from my palm burned, but I could feel the tie giving way. I shut off the energy in my palm, carefully pulling my wrists apart. The tie came undone like it was made of taffy.

I caught the rest of the plastic before it could hit the ground. I looked at Neeta. She too was holding her melted zip tie in one hand.

There was nothing left to do but start making a whole lot of noise. We would deal with the guards as they came. We were both at an advantage and a disadvantage. We were exactly where we wanted to be, but we were trapped inside a jail, behind secure doors, and there were guards galore, with no way out.

One step at a time.

I knew without speaking to Neeta that we would need to be as quiet as possible, although we could only be so quiet. The first thing to do would be to incapacitate the two guards, then move to open the cell door.

I held up my hand, palm out, ready to send a blast of light at the giant guard whose back was to me. Neeta did the same. I did my best to adjust for the man's size. He was truly the tallest, thickest man I'd ever seen. My normal blast wouldn't do it, but I also didn't want to kill him. This would be tricky.

Neeta glanced toward me, her eyebrows raised as if to ask, *Ready?*

I winked. At the same time, we both unleashed our light, our energy, the power that came from our core. We hit our targets at the same time, in the same spot, the dead center of their backs. Neeta's guy crumpled to the ground in a heap, out cold. Mine, not so much. He stumbled forward as if he'd been hit by a truck, but he didn't fall. Instead, he braced himself on the railing of the catwalk, his knees buckling but not hitting the ground.

"Finish him," Neeta said as she wrapped her hand

around the lock of the cell door.

The guard grunted, one hand reaching for the handgun at his waist. He began turning on the balls of his feet, one hand on his holster, the other on the railing as he braced himself.

Nervous energy coursed through me. The power was harder to control when my adrenaline spiked like this. I had to allow these feelings to move through me. The energy warmed in my palm, the blue flame dancing, ready to be released. I was afraid the blast would be too much, that the fear and anxiety spiking through my system would affect my magic, but there was nothing I could do. This was one of those us versus them moments. I let it go. The blast hit the enormous man square in his chest.

His face contorted as he tried to breathe, his cheeks going beet red, his eyes bulging. Panic flooded my chest. He collapsed backward, his mouth open in a silent scream.

Neeta stood at the cell door. She sent a pulse of energy through the lock which opened with a loud pop. She was out the door in a second, stepping over the crumpled men. She pressed her fingertips to the neck of the guard she'd blasted. "Alive."

Then she went to the other one, to the man I'd blasted twice, the man who was already blue in the face. She looked up at me, still standing in the center of holding cell 9, and shook her head. She straightened. "Come on, Miranda."

I watched Neeta take off down the catwalk, down the first set of stairs to the second level.

"Miranda." I heard her hiss somewhere below me.

I swallowed. My stomach, twisted into knots, was so sour I wanted to puke. But I didn't. I put one foot in front of the other until I was stepping over one guard, who still breathed, and then the other guard, who didn't. I pressed myself against the cell door as I made my way over and around him to keep myself as far away from him as possible. And I didn't look at him. I couldn't look at him. I couldn't let myself think for one second about what I'd done. I could think about that later. If I allowed myself to go there now, I'd dissolve and I'd never be able to move forward.

We still had a task. We still had lives to save.

Lives.

I squeezed my eyes shut as I descended the first set of open, metalwork stairs, gripping the railing so that I wouldn't fall. My eyes filled with tears that fell down my face in waves as soon as I opened them.

Neeta was already at the first cell, her hand sending a familiar pulse to open the door. "You go to the next one. I think we're being quiet enough, but our luck won't hold for long." She didn't look at me. Maybe she couldn't look at me. She just disappeared into the frigid dark of the first cell.

I did as I was told like some wind-up toy. The second cell held only one sleeping figure. I sent a small pulse through the lock, then slid the door wide. The woman was half-awake, her eyes partially open, but her face placid, dreamlike.

Crouching next to her, my breath caught in my throat. "It's you," I said to her, though she couldn't really hear me. The lady from Mississippi was in a deep stupor. This was the lady who'd really started it all. She was not the first woman to be taken into custody, but she was the first woman to be taken in after such a showy display. She'd been attacked, nearly raped on the street, then had accidentally killed her attacker when her magic had uncontrollably pulsed from her.

I shook her shoulders. "Miss? Miss, can you hear

me?"

The lady moaned, her head tossing from side to side. She'd been sweating, her dirty blonde hair sticking to the side of her face, her cheeks flushed a deep pink. Her body began thrashing and I worried she would hurt herself, so I placed both hands on the side of her face.

"Shh, it's okay. Everything is okay now." I spoke in the low, nurturing tone I remembered my own mother using to calm me when I was little. As I held the woman's face, cooing gentle words at her, my hands inexplicably warmed. I hadn't meant them to. There was no reason to use my magic at the moment, and I'd gained sufficient control of myself that at first, I didn't understand what was happening. Rather than burn the lady with my palms, I released her and scooted back.

Her eyes went wide. "Who are you?" she asked, her voice hoarse.

"I…" I paused, looking down at my hands. Did I just wake her up out of her stupor? "My name is Miranda. I've come with two others like us."

"To do what?" The look on her face was one of disbelief.

"To get you out. All of you. How do you feel?" The color on her cheeks was calming down, and her breathing had returned to normal.

"Better than I've felt in weeks." She moved up on her elbows.

I moved off the bed so she could sit up. I looked down at my hands. "I think my magic had something to do with that." I darted out of the cell to peer around the corner. "Neeta," I called.

Neeta poked her head out of the first cell. "I can't get this chick to wake up."

"Use your hands. Place them on the sides of her face. Just focus on her waking up. Trust me."

Neeta narrowed her eyes like she wasn't sure I was sane, then disappeared back into the cell.

I turned to see the lady from Mississippi standing and stretching her back.

"What's your name?" I asked her.

"Beth."

"All right, Beth." I smiled. "Time to help me wake up everyone else."

Five minutes later and we'd woken half the cell block. As we pulled ladies from their drug-induced stupors, they would join us in waking the next group. At this point, we had almost everyone with three cells to go.

I was heading into one of the last cells when above us, I heard the buzzing of the security doors. "They're coming," I said to no one in particular. Then, I shouted, "Crystal!"

Neeta shot in behind me, shoving me out of the way. She crouched on the bed next to her mother, her hands encircling Crystal's face. Tears fell from Neeta's eyes as she cradled her mother. I wanted to stay and watch, to make sure Crystal would wake, but we were now on the clock. I dashed to the next cell.

My heart almost stopped as I spied Ash inside, passed out in the same manner as everyone else.

I pivoted on one foot. "Beth, wake whoever is in the last cell."

We were so close, so close to having all the women conscious, so close to getting them the hell out of that pit, but the clock was now ticking and ticking fast. Whoever had just been buzzed through the first door was now being buzzed through the second. I could feel the reverberation of the door slamming open against the track. The women were powerful but untrained, untested.

My stomach lurched as I thought of the visions I had seen of rubble and destruction. Were they visions or just nightmares? My eyes blurred, but I blinked away the unwanted thoughts. There was only one thing to focus on at that moment, and it wasn't the asshats who were coming for us. It was Ash.

My beautiful Ash lay in the same feverish state as all the others. Her porcelain skin was flushed with fever, sweat trickling down her forehead, disappearing into her hairline.

I put my hand on the lock of the cell door, allowing one quick pulse to obliterate what stood between us. The door slid open without complaint. In the span of sixty seconds, I was at Ash's side.

"Ash." I dropped next to her, my knees slamming against the unforgiving concrete floor. "Ash, baby, I need you to wake up now."

When my flesh touched hers, I almost cried out. I'd forgotten how soft her skin was, how precious. I wanted to touch her again and again for the rest of my life. I pressed my lips against her forehead. "I'm so sorry this happened to you." She was so hot that a tremor of fear passed through me. A fever too high could cause brain damage or even death.

I whimpered, my lips still on her. "Wake up, Ash." I pressed my forehead against hers as I placed my hands on either side of her face. My palms warmed by the smallest degree, but she didn't stir. "Come on, baby." I tried again, but she remained in her state of delirium.

"Miranda." Neeta rushed into the cell.

I looked up to see her face streaked with tears. "Mom isn't waking up. What the fuck?" She was panicked, her face one of pure pain, her mouth hanging open as she stared at me for an answer. "Are we out of magic? Can you run out?"

"Ash isn't waking either. My hands are warm though." I pulled them away, staring at my palms.

"Maybe because they aren't magical, we can't wake them like the others." I glanced back down at Ash. Her state was unchanged. "We'll have to carry them out."

I stood, taking Neeta by the shoulders. Boots running down the catwalk above echoed all around us. Fear took hold of my body, cold sweat dripping down my back. "You and I have to blow an escape hole through the wall." I turned to look at the group of women gathered outside the cell. Each and every face was lined with worry. Some were visibly shaking, some holding onto each other, others turned to stare at the chaos above. "I need two of you to carry Crystal and two of you to carry Ash." They continued staring at me like lost children. "Now!"

A few of the women broke off to dive into Crystal's cell. Beth and two others moved forward to pull Ash off her cot and hold her between them.

"Come on." I pulled Neeta out to the common area. Shouts were now echoing above us. We had minutes, if even that, before the army of the gray-suited men was going to be down upon us. "If that was the interior of the prison, the way we came in, then that should be an exterior wall. Right?" I pointed to the solid wall of concrete blocks to the east of where we stood.

"Maybe." Neeta kept looking above. The men were now coming down the first set of stairs.

"Maybe is good enough for me." There was no time to wallow in the situation. I wanted nothing more than to have my arms around Ash in that moment, but if I did that, we'd never get out of here. It was time to move. "Let's hope the whole place doesn't collapse."

I held up both hands, Neeta doing the same, right alongside me. Together, we each sent four blasts at the wall. The sound was unholy. I'd never been to a demolition site, but I imagined the sound was the same.

The only difference being the people who brought down buildings wore hardhats and earplugs. Such luxuries were not for us.

We turned and crouched down, covering our heads with our arms as chunks of concrete flew around us. I choked through clouds of dust. When the jolt of the impact had settled, I glanced over at Neeta. She was covered in a fine white dusting of powder. Looking down at myself, I could see it was the same for me. When I opened my mouth, powder wafted down my throat, throwing me into a coughing fit.

We had been correct in our assessment. The hole we'd blasted revealed the dark night. The black pavement of the parking lot gleaming in the moonlight was the most beautiful sight I'd ever beheld.

That's when the bullets started flying.

"Go!" I screamed at the gathered women, my voice catching on the dust particles. Before turning to face the guards, I made sure I spied Crystal and Ash. They were there, suspended between our magical sisters.

Neeta and I took cover under one of the several long tables in the center of the common room. I grabbed Neeta by her shirt sleeve. "You need to get out of here. Make sure these women aren't being led to the slaughter and find Billie. I'll hold them here."

"Are you crazy?" Neeta pulled out of my grasp. "I'm not leaving you."

"One of us has to lead the women out of here, while one of us stays behind. Don't forget—don't die. If I see an out, I'll take it." I pushed her back as I launched myself out from under cover, my hands blazing. I knew in my heart only one of us was going to make it, and that Neeta should be the survivor. After what I'd done to the guard, I knew from the moment we descended the stairs that the one to sacrifice herself should be me.

All I wanted to see was Ash making it out of that hole. I knew Neeta would get them to safety, all of them. She'd find Billie, they'd get to Joey, and they would disappear. Neeta and Billie would make excellent teachers. Together, they would find a solution to this mess. I had to believe that.

Neeta garbled some sort of protest behind me, but it was too late. I was already on my feet, already moving toward the onslaught with my hands blazing blue flame.

The dust had not settled which helped. The poor visibility made it difficult for the guards to hit any targets. My lungs burned from the debris, but still, I breathed deeply. I had to. I could not let myself lose control no matter how afraid I was. This was my last chance to show these people that we were not to be feared, that we only wanted freedom, the chance to live our lives like any normal person. I could not afford to kill anyone else.

Two pulses of blue light came from behind me. I realized Neeta was laying down cover fire as she fled. I could hear the women crunching rubble as they ran out into the night.

I began my own assault, aiming for chests with pulses of energy meant only to stun.

Bullets whizzed past me. All I could hope for was that the women had made it out. I took out four, then five, then six guards, but there seemed to be an endless number streaming down the stairs, guns out. I felt like Neo in *The Matrix* and really wished I could contort my body like he could.

I began to back up as I blasted. Maybe, just maybe I could actually make it outside with the others. All I had to do was keep blasting as I moved.

I'd taken five steps back when a searing pain rocketed through my thigh. I almost buckled, almost went down on my knees, but I stayed upright. Having already been shot, I knew I had just taken a bullet in my leg. I had to keep going. They needed more time.

I took out seven more guards. Another shot hit me in the chest. This time, I knew it was bad. This was ten times worse than the shot I took in the side, with no one to help me close the wound. All the air seemed to vanish from my lungs. Unbearable pain wracked every breath. Wet warmth filled my bra, my shirt.

I tried with all my might to stay on my feet, but I dipped backward once, then twice, then fell hard on my backside. I sat in the rubble, the pain and dust choking the life out of me. With one hand still raised, I did my best to shoot my magic at the men who'd now stopped firing. I couldn't hold up my arm for long. My hand fell along with the rest of me. I stared at the ceiling, blood oozing from my body.

Life seemed to come to a complete stop around me. My right hand laid softly over the wound in my chest, warm stickiness sliding through my fingers. My left hand, no longer humming with any sort of magical energy, lay motionless on the cold concrete floor.

Rubble from the blown-to-bits wall cut into my back. I felt no pain, only registering the existence of the jagged pieces of wall. In fact, I felt no pain at all, anywhere in my body. This should have been alarming to me, but it wasn't. The world was going black around the edges, my vision tunneling, and for this I was grateful.

Everything was silent, calm, until it wasn't. Shouts echoed around me. The voices were so loud and so plentiful it was hard to ascertain where they came from. Blue light danced over my head, casting a glow on the stained white ceiling above me. The colors arced until they blended together to create undulating waves of blue and green.

This must be what the aurora borealis looks like.

A shield. Someone threw up a shield. Why hadn't I thought of that?

Then, hands were on me. I tried fighting because I couldn't see anything other than those dancing waves, and I didn't know who was trying to move me. I didn't want to move. I wanted to die right there, with no pain, only the pretty lights above me like a canopy.

Billie's pale and drawn face came parallel to my own. "I need you to help me, Miranda. Try to get up."

I rolled my head from side to side. I didn't want to get up, I really didn't. Everything had gone wrong from the second we came back to New Orleans. Our grand plans, foiled at every turn. They would all die, and I couldn't bear to watch it. Better to just expire right here.

Billie pushed my hand off my wound, covering it with her own.

A pain I'd thought long forgotten surged through my chest. My flesh burned with a sting I wanted to never experience again. I sucked in a breath, tears flowing past my temples into my hair.

"Stop," I said through gritted teeth. "Let me go."

"Not on your damn life. Now get the fuck up. Ash and the others are in a van heading at full speed toward the gates."

I tried focusing on her eyes, so brown they were almost black. "They'll never make it."

"A truck full of pissed-off, wide awake witches? Of course they'll make it."

"Is she awake?"

The blonde hair shook. "No, but she will be. Let's go."

I let Billie shove me into a sitting position. It was hard to see through the still stirred up dust, but the room was quiet. A few guards lay in heaps on the ground, the others, a dozen or so, stood with their hands up. Neeta and Beth stood side by side, palms out, light balls floating. The shield was a thing of beauty between us and danger.

Billie crouched behind me, hands hooking under my armpits. She hauled me to my feet, then held me in place while she snaked my arm around her neck, bracing me around the middle.

I slumped against her. Standing was hard. I'd lost a lot of blood, and the weakness in my legs was unlike anything I'd ever felt before. All I wanted to do was lie down and sleep.

Above us, that familiar buzzing of the security doors sounded ominous. I suppose the others looked up, but my neck would only loll to the side, so I had no idea what was coming for us now. Fear should have washed over me, but I was way past being afraid of anything.

Heels clicked on the catwalk over our heads. The walker moved fast down the metal walkway, feet moving with determination. Moments later, the same heels clicked down the steps, then crunched over debris.

"Stop right there. The shield will probably incinerate you." I heard Neeta as though she were talking through a dream. Only she wasn't talking to me. She was speaking to whoever had joined our horrible party.

"Your shield, though impressive, is unnecessary. The gate has been opened for your friends. You, too, will be allowed to leave untouched." The voice sounded familiar, much like Lou's gray-suited dad.

Neeta grunted. "I wouldn't say untouched. Two of our people have been drugged so deeply they're practically dead, and Miranda…" Neeta stopped, her voice cracking. "Look at her."

"Yes." The voice was maniacally calm. "Well, you're not the only ones who suffered casualties."

I thought my body was beyond the capacity to feel anything at the moment, but at the reminder of the man I'd killed, my stomach clenched, razor-like pains slicing through my chest.

"Why are you letting us go?" Neeta had resumed her in-charge attitude.

"Someone above me has ordered the release. It seems the three of you have stirred up quite the rebellion with your little video. And I'm sure what's happened here tonight has not gone unnoticed. I'm to direct you to a location." There was silence for a beat.

I tried raising my head to see what transpired, but my neck still wasn't obeying.

The man resumed. "Be there in three days with your delegation to negotiate terms."

"Delegation?" Neeta asked.

"You'll need representation. It's up to your coven, or whatever you call yourselves, to figure out who will represent you." There was spite in the man's voice. He was not happy about this turn of events.

"Whatever, man," Neeta said, right before I felt her bracing me from the other side. Together, Billie and Neeta held me between them, and together we shuffled over the rubble and out into the night.

Somehow, Joey's truck was parked on the asphalt, and then he was there, jogging toward us, taking me from Billie and Neeta and lifting me up into the air.

Billie was crying, Neeta was swearing, and Beth was there, too. Joey laid me in the backseat, my head in Beth's lap, my legs over Neeta.

"Shit, her leg." This was the last thing I heard before pain pulsed through my thigh, and the world went black.

Chapter Eighteen

I remember being in and out of consciousness. The way back to the highway was bumpy and just when I'd pass out, we'd hit a rut, and I'd be rocketed back into consciousness for a few awful seconds.

"Put her on the bed." Billie's small voice tumbled around the edges of my mind.

I was being carried in strong arms that had to be male.

"She needs a transfusion." Joey laid me down on a bed, the coverlet scratchy and rough under the backs of my arms.

I tried rolling over onto my side, but someone's hands kept me pinned in place.

"We can't take her to a hospital. No matter what that dick said, we don't know if we can fully trust them yet." Hands began stripping off my clothes. "We need lots of hot water, bandages, and alcohol. The gunshot wounds have all been closed and cauterized. The shots were clean—they went straight through—so we just need to clean her up, and make sure she doesn't get an infection. And acetaminophen, we need lots of that for everyone. She's young and strong, she'll live. This one is" —I felt pressure on my chest— "more shoulder than chest, so I don't think her lungs were punctured. If that were the case, she'd be coughing blood, and it's too far from her heart to be a concern there."

I wanted to be as optimistic as Billie, but I couldn't even open my eyes.

****

When I finally did open my eyes, I was under the covers, dressed only in my underwear, my skin sparkling clean, and bandages wrapped around my various wounds.

A bottle of water sat on the bedside table along with two pills sitting on a folded-up piece of tissue. I reached for the pills, popping them in my mouth, then guzzled down half the bottle of water.

Somehow, other than a general soreness, I felt like I might live to see another sunrise.

"Awake!" Billie walked out of the bathroom, drying her hands on a towel, a bright smile plastered across a tired face. She dropped the towel on the floor, swooping down on me, her arms wide. "How is my patient?"

I huffed against her shoulder. "Okay, I think." The words croaked past my dry throat. Images of the attack on the prison came rushing back. I pushed her away, my gaze moving around the empty room. "Where is Ash, and everyone else? What's happened? Where are we?" The questions came in a rush.

"Whoa, don't freak out. We have a block of four rooms. Most of the girls are sleeping in the last two, Joey went out to get dinner for everyone, and Ash and Crystal are next door with Neeta."

"Billie, tell me how she is, how they are." I shoved Billie back as gently as I could, swinging my feet out from under the blankets.

I stood too quickly, my knees buckling, my head swimming.

"Miranda, you can't just stand up like that. You're doing well, but you still lost a lot of blood. It's going to be days, maybe even longer before you can run around like you haven't a care." She grabbed me by the waist, pushing me back onto the bed. "We can go in to see them, but we have to stand by degrees. The first step is sitting here with your feet on the floor. So, sit here and breathe, and I'll tell you what's happened."

She sat down next to me. "Ash and Crystal are

doing okay. Not great, but like you, they're going to survive. We brought down their fevers with ice and cold water. We literally put them one after the next in baths filled with ice water and forced acetaminophen down their throats. It took a couple of hours, but the fevers broke. They both threw up a few times, but once they started doing that, they both began coming out of their drug stupors. We've tried to keep them hydrated and resting. Neeta hasn't left their sides. She was in there with them, while Joey stayed in here with you, and I ran back and forth."

My head lolled onto her shoulder. "I knew you'd make a great nurse." I thought of Ash nearly dying. Crystal, too. They hadn't been a part of this; they hadn't deserved any of it. Not that the witches had, either, but the two of them hadn't even been magical. They'd just been swept up in the drama because of their connection to us. Crystal, with her love for Neeta, was so caring and kind. Ash and her sweet, frank nature. Her eyes that could see so far into my soul. I'd felt seen, felt known, the first time she pierced me with her stare. My chest tightened, my throat burning, as tears spilled from my eyes onto Billie's shoulder.

"Should we go see them?" she asked.

I nodded against her. "First, tell me what happened at the jail."

Billie groaned. "That's a little harder to explain. I guess our video went viral, like mega-viral, and women all over the globe not only saw it but have taken our lessons and words to heart. Our guess is that we're now too powerful a combined force to be quieted away, so the government wants to negotiate some sort of terms with us. We'll find out tomorrow."

"I'm going."

"Absolutely not. You're too weak. Neeta, Beth,

and I will go. It's already been decided by the group."

I raised my head, leveling Billie with one glare. "If you think I'm not going to this meeting after everything we've been through, think again. Beth is welcome, but it's the three of us, always."

Billie shook her head. She looked too tired to argue. "Neeta said you'd be stubborn about it, that you've become more stubborn than her."

"I wouldn't go that far."

Billie laughed.

"Now, help me up so I can see Ash."

****

Minutes passed before I made it to the door, sweat breaking out on my upper lip. More minutes passed while we shuffled down the walk of the motel to the door right next to ours. The motel had a very Fleur-de-lis type vibe, everything 1970s, oranges and browns, paint peeling off doors and walls.

When Billie finally reached out a hand to open the motel room door and push it open, I gasped.

There was Ash sitting half up on one of the beds, the one farthest from the door. Her face and lips were blanched white—she looked like a ghost. The only color on her face was the red rims around her eyes, but when the door opened and she saw me, she smiled. That smile almost broke the dam within me. That smile made everything I'd been through in the last weeks, everything we'd been through, worth it.

"Hey," she croaked, her throat dry, no doubt, from days of being unconscious.

"Hi." I pushed off Billie, wanting more than anything to walk the rest of the way myself. Crystal's bed was empty. The light was on in the bathroom, and the shower was running, so I guessed she must be well enough to wash up. That made me happy.

Neeta stood, leaning against the bathroom door, no doubt ready to help her mom if she needed it.

"What happened to you?" Ash tried pushing herself up farther, but her elbow gave out and she slumped back to where she was, her face crossed in consternation.

"I was shot three times. That'll really take it out of you, let me tell you." I managed to make my way to the foot of her bed, sucking in my breath with every step. Everything hurt. When I sank onto the bed next to her and she took my hand, most of the pain melted away.

Her chin wobbled as she brushed back my hair with her free hand.

How could I get these words out?

"I'm fine, and I love you," I said, staring into her eyes. I trailed a finger over the freckles on the bridge of her nose. "And I'm so sorry this happened to you. It's all my fault—your being here."

Ash squeezed her eyes shut, her head shaking back and forth. "This is in no way your fault. I'm just so glad we made it out. All of us. And..." She opened her eyes. "Billie said this might be over?" She sounded so hopeful.

I wanted more than anything to shout that our nightmare was, indeed, over, but I couldn't lie, not to her. Instead, I shrugged. "Maybe. I guess we'll see what happens tomorrow."

She nodded as she held my hands in both of hers. "And I love you." Her gaze was intent on mine. This stare used to feel like impending disaster—fire alarms or flares seen from a distance. Now the look was calming—like waves crashing onto a beach.

****

I stayed curled up with Ash for the rest of the day. Crystal came out, looking better than all of us combined, and got back in bed. The three of us watched game shows and ate soup, delivered to us steaming hot by Joey.

That night, Neeta slept next to her mom, the four of us enjoying a sort of invalid sleepover. Billie and Joey took the room I'd been in. The rest of the women had crammed themselves into the other two rooms.

The morning of the meeting, I was up early. A human being can only sleep so much, even when they're full of bullet holes. I took a shower, washing up the best I could with stiff limbs, then dressed in a clean sweatshirt and jeans purchased for me at the local superstore. I blew dry my hair, leaving it down and wavy for the first time in a good while. I wasn't exactly sure who we were meeting with but wanted to make sure I looked the best that was possible given the circumstances. I didn't want to give them the satisfaction of seeing me beat down.

There was a tap on the door right before Neeta stuck her head in. "Hey, I want to rinse off before we head out. You done?" She was whispering, which told me our roomies were still asleep.

"Yep, I'm going to stretch my legs outside. Check on Billie. Come out when you're done."

I wasn't sure where we were, but guessed we had to be in Shreveport. I had never thought to even ask. The motel was the same one-story, linear design as the Fleur, but this one, I noticed for the first time, had a western theme to it. There was a cowboy on the sign, pointing down at the rooms as he smiled a giant smile at passersby. Wagon wheels dotted the parking lot, and the planters were in the shape of cowboy boots.

I knocked on Billie's door. She opened it almost immediately, slipping out next to me on the sidewalk. "Joey is still asleep. Where's Neeta?"

"Quick shower."

"Cool, we should probably get going." She leaned

against the closed door, her arms crossed over her chest. She wore the same jeans I did, only her sweatshirt was blue, while mine was green.

When Neeta came out only moments later, she too wore the same jeans, and a yellow sweatshirt.

"We look like a box of crayons," I said.

Billie giggled. "There weren't a lot of options at the big box store up the road. I did the best I could."

"Are we ready to do this?" Neeta asked.

"Shouldn't we tell them all we're leaving?" I shuffled on the walk. Although I was ready to get on with whatever this meeting was, I was nervous all the same. "What if this is a trap?"

Billie shrugged. "I left Joey a long note. I'm tired of saying goodbye. And I don't think this is a trap, do you? This feels different. Our video is all over the news and no one has bothered us." She looked toward Neeta, who nodded.

"I agree. This doesn't feel like a trap. Anyway, we're not going alone."

Just then, as if on cue, the doors to the other two rooms we'd rented opened, and out streamed the rest of the witches. There were over twenty of us in total, Beth included. She stood at the front of the group.

I surveyed the strong-looking women. "Okay, then. I guess we're piling into Joey's truck?"

****

Pile in, we did. Billie, Neeta, Beth, and I crammed into the front seat of the cab, while four others crammed into the back seat. All the rest jumped in the bed of the truck. We didn't have far to go, and for this I was grateful. I couldn't imagine how strange we must have looked, not to mention, I was pretty sure this was illegal. More legal trouble was one thing we didn't need.

The address given to Neeta took us to a rather

nondescript parking lot.

"A diner?" Billie, who was driving the truck, peered over the steering wheel and out the window. "Are they serious?"

"Seems a little strange, I'll grant you that." Neeta, crammed in next to Billie, ran a hand over her mouth as she, too, stared out the window.

I had to agree. The setting was nothing short of bizarre, especially given the events of the past several weeks. To now have it all possibly end at a retro diner, complete with a shiny silver awning and bright neon signs, was a little unsettling.

Even more unsettling was the fact that there were no patrons. Save for the truck and two large black SUVS, the windows so tinted it was impossible to see inside, the lot was empty.

Billie drifted into one of the many open spaces, this one directly in front of the huge window. We could clearly see inside the nearly empty diner. The kitchen beyond the turquoise counter was dark. Three men in black suits occupied stools at the counter, their backs to us. Each man looked identical from the back with those high and tight haircuts. From the right ear of each man ran a wire that disappeared inside the white collar of the shirts they wore under their black suit jackets.

Sitting at a table, a booth, right in the middle of the diner, were two men. One was Lou's gray-suited dad, and the other was someone I'd seen on television a hundred times.

"Is that?" I leaned forward, my hands on the dash, narrowing my eyes to get a clearer look.

"I think it is." Beth sat wedged between me and the truck door, which she opened to jump out of. She stepped onto the pavement, her head on a swivel, scanning the parking lot. "I don't think there's anyone else around."

I squirmed out after her, Billie and Neeta getting out on the other side.

I looked at the gaggle of women still in the bed of the truck. "You guys stay put but stay alert." There was a general murmur of assent.

Billie and I joined Beth and Neeta by the door of the diner. The men inside had seen us but didn't make it seem like they had.

We stood in a semi-circle looking at each other like we hadn't a clue what to do next.

Neeta, her hands on her hips, flicked a gaze inside the diner then fixed her stare on me. "If you're feeling up to it, you should be the one to speak for us, Miranda."

"What?" I hadn't been expecting that. Speaking for an entire group of women, 95% of whom I didn't know, was a daunting task, and one I was wholly unprepared for.

"You were the first of our group to get your powers. You were the first to fear for your life, the first to have to flee your home, and the first to give everything up. You're so young, and what's happened to you was so deeply unfair that I think you would be the one most able to articulate what we've been through." Her warm brown eyes gazed at me with such love I had to bite my lip to keep from getting emotional. I didn't want these men to see me cry.

I thought about what Neeta was saying. I had been through a lot, but it wasn't any more than any of us had been through. "Beth has been through a lot, and you, and Billie. We've all fought for survival." I glanced away. I did feel up for it. I felt more than up for a confrontation with these men who'd taken everything from us, but not alone. We were only strong when we were together. "I'll lead the conversation, but I need the three of you at my back, at the ready to tell your own stories, to help guide me in what's right for all of us." I held out my hand. "This is cheesy, but let's do it anyway."

Billie laid her long-fingered, pale hand over mine.

Neeta laid her small, brown hand over Billie's.

Beth laid her hand, nails chipped and broken, over Neeta's.

"Let's do this, bitches." Leave it to Neeta to make us all laugh.

Chapter Nineteen

The inside of the diner was hot. The warmth felt good as the morning had been chilly. I pushed up the sleeves of my green sweatshirt.

I walked in first, over black and white linoleum, toward the booth that held Lou's dad and the man we'd been shocked to see. The older man, his hair white, his face lined with age, gave one, curt nod to Lou's dad who immediately slid out of the booth and onto a stool next to the three other men I now realized were Secret Service.

"Please ladies, sit." The man with white hair gestured at the empty bench seat across from him.

The man with the white hair was the President of the United States.

My hands shook, not with my powers, but with nerves. I clasped them together as Billie moved around me to slide in first. I went in next, Neeta last. Beth stood a little behind us. The president didn't seem unnerved by us at all. He merely sat, his hands folded on top of the table, a placid, serene look on his face. It was not quite a smile, but close.

"I hope everyone is okay, after the events of the other night." He looked into each of our faces in turn, giving each of us an equal amount of attention. He was a politician, all right.

I took a deep breath. "Well, I was shot three times, and all the women who were imprisoned were drugged, two of whom are non-magical, and they nearly died from the drugs. So, I guess we're doing as well as can be expected." I kept my voice even. I didn't want to sound menacing or condescending. I just wanted to sound like I was imparting information, nothing more.

The president cleared his throat. "Yes, well, it's

my understanding that a guard was killed that night." He paused, letting his words, which were a punch to my gut, sink in. "What I propose, in the spirit of moving forward, is that we start fresh from right here. There is a lot that I was not made aware of until recently. Some bad decisions were made." Here, he paused again to look at the back of Lou's dad.

Lou's dad stiffened as if he knew the president was staring a hole through his gray suit jacket.

"Now that I'm fully in the loop, practices will change. Which is why we're all here today." He reached down to his seat, then placed a beige folder on the table, which he tapped with his index finger. "I'd like to propose a database where witches, or whatever the approved vernacular is, will register. You ladies will be able to live your lives as normal—work, go to school, whatever you like. There will be new laws put in place that will deal with magic use. Of course, magic will not be permitted to be used to hurt others. If it is, the user will be prosecuted. Magic cannot be used on public transportation, et cetera. It's all in here. Of course, this is preliminary. More laws could be added in the future."

I leaned back against my seat, glancing at Billie and then Neeta. They both gave tiny shakes of their heads.

I glanced down at my hands, still clasped in my lap. Before they shook from nervousness at sitting across from such a powerful man. Now they shook from anger. I bit the inside of my lip, clasping my hands tighter together.

"I think we can agree that some of the laws will be fine. We'd never advocate using our magic to hurt people. Magic can be a weapon like anything else. And not using magic on things like airplanes is a given. But the database. I think that's where you lost us."

"I understand. No one likes the idea of being tracked, but let's be real for a second, ladies." The president leaned forward over the table like he was imparting some sort of secret. "Everyone is tracked to some extent."

"No offense, Mr. President, but we're not stupid. We know that. If there is some kind of informal tracking that goes on, or some unofficial database you keep, I guess there isn't much we can do about that, but as for signing our names to a document, absolutely not. It won't happen." I had to press my fingernails into the flesh of my palm to keep my cool. Here was little me going head-to-head with the President of the United States while several men, who were surely strapped to the heavens, sat not five feet away.

The president inclined his head to the side as he stared hard into my eyes. He refolded his hands, the look on his face unchanging.

I held his gaze, refusing to look away. I felt like this was part of it. If I looked away, he wouldn't concede.

The clock over the cash register ticked away, seconds, then minutes. When I thought I might buckle, might actually have to look away, one side of his mouth quirked up into a half smile.

"This is only the beginning of negotiations, but I agree to cross out the database. For now."

****

When we arrived back at the western-themed motel, all I wanted to do was run to Ash. We were finally free. Free from persecution, free from fear. At least for now. I was sure there would be unforeseen problems, that someone, somewhere would start some shit. It was so hard to have nice things in this world, but for now, I felt safe. I didn't have to run; I didn't have to hide.

Billie pulled into a spot, and the women streamed

out of the back. They, too, were free to go back to their lives.

Ash, Crystal, and Joey all sat in plastic chairs in front of our rooms, cups of coffee in each hand. As soon as we parked, they all stood.

I limped over to Ash, my body still sore, but my spirit freer than it had been in a while. She stood with one hand on the back of her chair, the other wrapped around her coffee. She was still weak, too, but already she had more color, her eyes as bright as they were the first time we met.

"How'd it go?" she asked, holding out her cup to me.

"Great." I took the cup, handing it off to Joey, then took her face in my hands. "Everything is going to be wonderful now."

I didn't even care that we were surrounded. I pressed my lips to hers right there on the walk of that motel. This kiss was everything I'd longed for since leaving New Orleans. Shutting out the world was easy. I focused on Ash and how she felt in my arms—soft, warm, like home.

Her lips devoured mine as hungrily as mine devoured hers. She wound her arms around my waist, pulling me even closer, the kiss deepening as our mouths opened and our tongues slid against each other.

My hands slid farther into her hair, my fingers winding through her locks.

"Um, excuse us." I heard Billie speak through the fog of my longing for Ash.

"Like you're one to talk." Neeta was ribbing her. "Do you remember the night at the Fleur when you and the Empire State Building were practically having sex against the jukebox in full view of everyone?"

I pulled away from Ash right before I started

laughing. "That's right. You can't talk."

"Well, fine, but we do have one more thing to discuss."

"What?" All I wanted to discuss was when we were leaving for New Orleans.

"Miranda is still only sixteen. So, which one of us is going to adopt her? I doubt she wants to go back to Colorado." Billie made a good point. As much as I wanted to pretend I was all grown up, I still had a couple of years, and finishing school was important.

"I am." Crystal reached out a hand, pulling me over to her. "I'll reach out to your parents to get the ball rolling, but we need to set some ground rules. The door to your room stays open when you have guests, and I expect you home by ten on weekdays, midnight on weekends. You need to finish school, young lady."

"Really? You want to adopt me?" My voice cracked.

"Really. My townhome has three bedrooms. One for me, you, and Neeta."

"What about Billie?" I craned my neck to see Billie entwined in Joey's arms.

He smiled at me, before glancing down at her. "Billie is moving in with me and working at the bar while she goes back to school."

"Okay." Tears spilled down my cheeks. "I like this plan."

****

We said goodbye to the women from the jail, but not before making sure each one had a place to go. They all promised to keep in touch.

Beth could not return to Mississippi after what happened, so she bought a bus ticket to go stay with her grandmother in North Dakota. We gave her the longest hug goodbye.

The six of us—me and Ash, Billie and Joey, and Neeta and Crystal, all packed in Joey's truck for the five-hour drive back home.

Home.

I thought I'd known what home was, but I hadn't had a clue. Not until I met these people, people who'd been nothing but strangers to me, who'd seemed so odd, so otherworldly, and who were now so deeply a part of me that I didn't know if I'd ever survive without them.

Epilogue

Six Months Later

Neeta and Billie sat cross-legged. The empty, decrepit house on Magazine Street was the only building with rent we could afford. And for our purposes, the four walls were perfect.

I walked in through the screen door, so holey it looked like Swiss cheese. In my hand, I held a letter from Estes Park.

"Hey." Neeta leaned back on her hands. "We were talking paint colors. I think we should pick something neutral and calming, but Billie is insisting on pink. You're the tie vote."

"Definitely not pink."

Billie grunted her disappointment.

I held up the envelope. "I finally heard back from Aunt Bea."

Neeta and Billie both leaned forward, eyes wide, mouths closed.

"She needed a minute before she responded. She says she's still processing what happened, how Lou was able to influence her magically. Anyway, she isn't upset with us one bit. More upset with herself. She apologized to me for like, ten pages. She was a little hurt that Crystal's adopted me, but happy that everything is going so well. She wants to visit, and she fully endorses the school and our use of the grimoire. The only thing she said in regard to that was just because we have the grimoire does not mean our learning is at an end. We should always be seeking more knowledge."

Billie smiled, an eyebrow shooting up. "Thank goodness. I was worried about her and about how she'd respond to the school."

"This is great news," Neeta agreed. "Now we can move forward without worry. I'm thinking gray for the walls."

"Gray is so boring." Billie fell to her side in dramatic fashion. "Can we at least agree on blue? You know, an actual color?"

I just laughed as I left them to argue.

Ash was waiting for me to pick her up from work.

We were home, and our future was one of infinite possibilities.

The End

A.D. BRAZEAU

Evernight Teen ®

<u>**www.evernightteen.com**</u>